The Expectant Widow

The Expectant Widow

Jenny Dawson

Published by Profic 2016

Written by Jenny Dawson

copyright©2016, by Jenny Dawson

Cover deigned by Melody Simmons

Profic

www.profic.dk

profic@mail.dk

CHAPTER ONE

Mona Mol's hands went numb, her fingers barely able to feel the broom handle. Her mouth went dry, dizziness overtaking her brain. The spring sunshine streamed in through the family room window, the heat suddenly cooking the churning nausea in her gut. With her stomach heavy and her head light, Mona felt as if she was being torn apart.

Oh no, she thought to herself, *not again, please not again!*

Mona leaned on the broom, pushing it against the pine floorboards for support. But the bristles bent and Mona lurched forward, barely keeping on her feet. Her knees buckling, Mona reached out, her body folding into the sofa. The room was silent around her, but Mona's mind was echoing with questions and concerns.

Must have been something we had for breakfast, Mona reassured herself. *Could the butter have turned? Was there a leak in the blueberry jam's mason jar?*

Mona thought about Nathan, working at the Abernathy's well. *Is he sick too? He'll be furious with me, and with every right!*

A cluster of knocks on the unfinished oak door, sending ripples of worried vibration through her body, stiffening her spine and sending her stomach to lurch up toward the bottoms of her quivering lungs.

Mona tried to call out but couldn't, her legs unable to push her up and across the room. She had no idea who was on the other side of that door, or what business brought them to her home, but she knew it had something to do with her sudden sickness.

It wasn't just something from breakfast. Mona had endured these before, always hoping they were a trick of the mind. But the attacks were real, she knew then, premonitions of terror, heralds of great sorrow. They'd always struck just before moments of crisis in her life; the day Jack died, the day the schoolhouse burned down.

Another cluster of knocks shattered her sad recollection, and a muffled voice was almost recognizable from the other side, calling her name.

"Missus Mol? It's Sheriff Baller, Mrs. Mol, Adams County Sheriff's Department."

Mona's legs reacted instinctively, carrying her to the door as her trembling hand reached out to the iron knob. It clicked as she turned it, the door heavy as she pulled it open in front of her. Sheriff Ken Baller stood tall in his tan uniform, his brown mustache over his flat frown.

"Sheriff," Mona managed to say.

"Mona Mol," he said, confirming her identity. "I'm here with some bad news, I'm afraid." Mona stepped back, the sheriff entering but leaving the front door open behind him "It's your husband, a Nathan Mol, of this address." Mona only nodded, waiting to hear the news she was already able to guess. "Well, Mrs. Mol, it seems there was an accident at the home of Bob and Lorraine Abernathy, in the well your husband was digging."

The air was sucked from Mona's lungs and they were unable to draw in anymore. Her skin went cold, stuck by a million invisible needles. And that nausea kept rising in her gut, ever-threatening to explode from her cramping face, a new and twisted mask of unspeakable sorrow.

"Seems the hole collapsed around him," Sheriff Baller went on, his voice as low and soft and comforting as his position would allow. "By the time the ambulance got to him, it was too late."

Mona fell back, the sheriff's strong hand grabbing her upper arm and easing her onto the arm of the sofa. Mona's imagination exploded with hideous visions of Nathan, so tall and strong, pick or shovel in his hands as those muddy walls closed in on him. She couldn't help but see the panic in his expression, eyes going wide as the Earth swallowed him whole.

"Did he … did he suffer?"

After a long and terrible pause, Sheriff Baller cleared his throat. "It seems he had enough time to drop his pick and try to climb out. There is … some evidence of a struggle."

Tears pushed up out of Mona's eyes, a gasp erupting beneath them. Mona could see him reaching out, teeth gritted, hands outstretched, those muddy walls falling in around him, their weight pushing him back, mud filling his mouth and throat.

Mona herself couldn't breathe, and Sheriff Baller reached up to the radio transmitter clipped to the epaulette of his uniform shirt. "HQ, this is Baller at the Mol house, I'm going to need an ambulance here on the double."

Mona reached out, shaking her head. She wanted to reassure him that it wasn't necessary, that she would be fine.

But she couldn't. She couldn't speak a work nor draw a breath, and before she could fear for her own life, it seemed to come to a sudden and abrupt end, darkness and stillness overwhelming her.

*

Mona had come around in the ambulance, but by then the paramedics insisted on taking her to Adams County General for tests. The staff were all very friendly, though she spent hours waiting for their attention. After urinating into a cup, giving blood, and enduring a few more humiliating tests, Mona sat on the hard metal examination table, long and rectangular like a bed. After another hour, the Englischer doctor, the African American Dr. Marjorie Larson, glanced at Mona and then at a metal clipboard in her hand.

"I'm sorry to hear about your husband, m'dear. But I wouldn't be surprised if what's wrong with you is stress, complicated by grief. Have you ever heard of post traumatic stress disorder?"

"But … the attack happened, started really, before I heard the news. It always hits just before."

"Always? How often does this happen?"

Mona shrugged. "It hasn't happened in years, really, I was beginning to wonder if it wasn't all in my head."

9

The doctor chuckled. "It is, in a way, and your body too." Reading Mona's confusion, the doctor explained, "Have you ever flinched, Mona? Sometimes we anticipate danger, our bodies can sense it. It's purely instinctive, physiological."

"Physio — ?"

Doctor Larson offered a reassuring smile. "Go home and get some rest, dear, you'll be all right."

So much for the Englischers and their great Western medicine, Mona couldn't help but think. Mona wasn't sure what was causing her spells, but she knew it was more than just her body or her mind.

But Mona was relieved to see the familiar faces waiting for her in the hallway. Lucas Tillerman loomed over his family, big arms outstretched. "Daed," Mona said wearily as she fell into his chest. "Mamm," she said to Betty Tillerman, her gentle hand on Mona's arm.

"My child," Betty said, "are you unwell?"

"Fine, Mamm," Mona said, glancing down at her kid sister Charlotte's round, pink face. "Charlie, you needn't have come too."

Charlie shrugged, at ten years old a full decade younger than Mona. "I'm sorry about what happened … to Nathan, I mean."

"She knows what you mean," Lucas said sternly, turning to Mona, "and we all feel as Charlie does, of course."

"A tragic turn," Betty said, her brows arched in sad sympathy.

"T'was God's will," Lucas corrected his wife, "as in all things. We are blessed to have even a small part in His great plan, let us not forget. And whatever time we have on this Earth to please him is a gift."

"Yes, Husband."

"Some are blessed with greater gifts than others," Lucas said, "more time or less, but all of life is a rare gift." Mona's head dipped, her tired heart aching again, her mind beginning to pulse with visions she could neither control nor ignore. Lucas seemed to read her expression, and he added, "He was a good man, worthy of the gift of life, and he honored God and the community admirably."

Mona nodded. She could not disagree, nor much else. Betty said, "You'll stay with us tonight, in your old room." Mona wanted to refuse, to insist on the independence she'd worked so hard for. But she simply couldn't, and Mona began to wonder if she'd ever be able to return to the life she'd known, that she'd been blessed with and which she'd earned.

11

Or so she'd thought.

But Mona knew her life would never be the same, and she had no idea what was awaiting her, what God had planned for her, or whether she'd survive it.

*

The Mol house rang with Ruth's wailing, her throat splitting as her sorrow poured out of twisted lips. Her face in her hands, Ruth was bent forward on the chair at the kitchen table. Behind her, William Mol stood solemn, erect, shoulders back in the face of his grief.

"You must forgive my wife," William finally said, Mona standing awkwardly several feet away from both of them. "We know you too must be grieving." Mona nodded but could say nothing, even as her mind and heart clamored. William went on, "What a terrible blow you to you, and so early in life."

Nodding, Mona finally managed to say, "At least the shock has passed."

"Our only child," Ruth screeched out before another group of gut-wrenching sighs. "My darling boy!"

"Control yourself, Wife! Would you have the Lord doubt your faithfulness?"

"The Lord," Ruth repeated, as if in disbelief, "the Lord?" She sat open-mouthed, unable to process the questions that were burning in her soul, the unfathomable horror of the turn her life had taken.

William said to Mona, "My son was working when he died, as you know. I hope you can take some comfort in that, as we do."

Mona nodded, the picture of the two suffering parents raising more questions than it ever could answer. They were to two faces of grief in Mona's imagination: Ruth's wail came from the utter depths of her tormented soul, the sound of a million angels screaming; her husband's sadness took a different shape, stopped up in him with such density and hardness that even a single tear would be hard-pressed ever to find release.

And Mona knew there was nothing she could do to ease their pain anymore than she could ease her own. Because Mona's pain was of a different sort, one she couldn't understand nearly so easily as she could the pain of others. There was that hollowness ringing in her soul, one she marked as Nathan's new absence. But she could hardly be sure, as they hadn't really been apart in the ten years they'd known each other. She'd never known this feeling, but she had the nagging suspicion that it was only going to get worse.

*

The traditional three-day period before an Amish funeral passed slowly for Mona. She tried to help her mamm around the house, but it was little distraction. Mona was haunted by melancholy, and nobody around her had much reason to wonder about its inspiration. Betty in particular, being Mona's mamm, could sympathize for her daughter. But there was nothing she nor anybody could do to bring Nathan back and everybody knew it, Mona especially.

Even a visit from Olivia Schmidt could bring Mona little solace. "Ross sends his best," she said to Mona, a comforting hand on her arm.

Mona smiled. "I'm grateful," was all she could say and all she needed to say. Both young women knew there were very good and very terrible reasons for Mr. Schmidt's absence. As per Amish tradition, he as a married man was helping to dig the grave and would be a pal bearer. But there was more to it than that, something neither woman wanted to recognize. One woman's husband was still alive, after all, something the other didn't need to be reminded of just yet.

"Nathan's a good man," Mona said, "and a good friend. I'm glad you've found each other, Liv, I'm glad that you're so blessed."

Liv tried to smile. "Have you heard from Gil?" Mona shook her head. "Strange," Liv went on, "you three have always been so close."

"He's being respectful," Mona said, "that's all. You know how much he worries about … matters of appearance. He wouldn't want anybody to think the lesser of him to come rushing to me in such a time."

"Think the lesser," Liv said, "you mean … that he's in love with you? Everybody already knows that, Mona."

"Liv!"

Liv rolled her eyes. "It's okay, Mona, nobody thinks any the lesser of him, of either of you."

But Mona needn't have said, "Anyway, he's helping to dig the grave, along with the Roland brothers. If only those two been there at the Abernathy's to help dig that well, as they should have been."

"Their buggy broke a wheel on the way to the Abernathy house, it wasn't their fault. I know they feel just terrible about what happened. As pal bearer, they'll have their chance to shake his hand before saying goodbye. Gil won't even have that chance, being a single man still. And at our age."

Mona tried to shrug it off. "He's a very exceptional man, you know that. He hasn't found the woman God intends for him, a woman of equal qualities. He's an artist, after all."

Liv nodded. "One of his creations stands in my own front yard," Liv said, "that great grizzly stands like some wooden protector, as if the tree had grown in that very spot! Working with that chainsaw, I can't hep but fear for his safety."

Mona nodded. "He's quite capable, and skilled."

"So was Nathan." A sudden quiet settled over the living room, but Liv was quick to say, "Oh, Mona, I didn't mean to say that — "

"No, no, it's okay, Liv. You're right, Nathan was capable and worthy, what happened … it was an accident, and they could happen to anybody, at almost any time."

Liv shook her head. "Why was he digging alone? He should have waited for the others to get there."

"You know Nathan, he was … determined, so hard-working."

Liv nodded. "It's not really what's important though, is it? Strange how hard we work, with our farming and our toil — "

"The better to avoid the distractions of the modern world, Liv."

"But there are other things besides work, eh? Family, love, God."

"He was a good husband," Mona said, "and would have been a good daed if God had seen fit to allow it."

"Of course he would have been, Mona, I didn't mean to suggest otherwise. I understand your grief, I surely don't mean to make it any worse."

Mona tried to ignore the discontent broiling inside her, festering and spreading. She looked into the sympathetic brows of her oldest friend. It was almost easy to crack a tiny smile. "I'm sorry to snap at you, Liv, I know you didn't mean anything. You're a sweet girl and a dear friend." A cold stone sank in Mona's gut as she said aloud what she couldn't help but think. "I believe I may need your friendship now; and soon enough I may need it more than ever before."

"And you'll always have it," Liv said, matching Mona's bittersweet smile with one of her own.

*

Only a few short hours later the shed phone rang behind the Tillerman house. Lucas answered, and he solemnly told his daughter that she had a caller.

Mona knew instantly who it was.

17

"Gil," she said, once inside the rotting little wooden shed.

"Mona, I'm so sorry about Nathan."

"That's kind of you, Gil, thank you."

After a somber silence, Gil said, "I'd have come by, but I know how things must be for you now, visitations of all sorts, preparations — "

"You're carrying your own weight as far as that's concerned, Gil. What a labor it must be, to dig a grave for such an old and dear friend."

"He was dear, very, but no more so to me than he was to you. He was your husband, after all." A reflective moment passed, Mona wondering what her old friend was thinking before the small, metallic voice said, "What about the Mols? They must be beside themselves."

Mona nodded, though she knew that he could not see it over the phone. She never got used to using that contraption, and she hoped she never would have to. Gil went on, "I have to get back to my chores, they're piling up while I'm otherwise indisposed." After a knowing silence, Gil added, "I'll see you … in a day or so then."

"Yes, Gil, and thank you for calling."

"If there's anything you need, you'll give me a call?"

"Of course I will, Gil, yes."

Gil paused. "I mean it, Mona."

"I know you do, Gil," was all she could think to say, "I know, and I will."

But Mona knew she wouldn't.

*

The first night in Mona's old bedroom was filled with echoing disquiet. Crickets chirped in the Indiana fields, as they always did and always would, beardtongue pollen drifting through the opened window, gently pushing back the white curtains. But in Mona's ears, the crickets were off-key, their continuous monotone more screeching and invasive to her ears than it ever had been before. And the scent of the wildflowers, once perfumed and delightful, was rancid in Mona's nostrils, resting on the back of her tongue like a fungus.

The house creaked, still settling after so many years.

Mona had to wonder, *Didn't I ever leave here? Didn't I grow up and get married to Nathan, as everyone always said we would? Didn't I move out and start a family of my own? Didn't I at least try?*

After saying her prayers to praise God for protecting her family and friends, and to bid that He see Nathan's soul to a place of ease and tranquility, beside the still waters, her mind and her prayer began to wander.

I know You are great and good, Lord, sympathetic to our needs. And I've never questioned You, even when you took Jack to be with you at such an early age. You created him and us all, and the cancer which took him from us. You made the Earth that swallowed up my Nathan, just when we were looking ahead to the life we'd planned for so long, since we were children.

Why, Lord? I know You have your purpose, but if I could just know what reason You had, what purpose his death would have in Your plan ... I don't mean to set terms or limits on You or Your ways. I never have and I never will. But this, taking Nathan in such a manner, there must be a reason! And knowing that reason, I can only hope that it might heal this strange hollowness inside me now. For I am Your child, Lord, Your creation, and this hollowness ... is that Your creation too, Lord, Your plan? Or am I falling short of the mark, Lord, sinning despite my purest efforts to honor you with my every step, my every word and my every breath? You know the secrets of my heart, Lord, and You know that I am not perfect in too many ways to count. You already know them all, each and every one. We both know I am small and frail, Lord, and only in your shadow am I made whole and worthy. But am I so unworthy, have I fallen so short that Nathan had to pay with his very life?

20

Or did Nathan himself sin, in ways I do not know? Are there things about Nathan I do not know, things which You do not want me to know? No, Lord, it cannot be that. He was a good man, faultless in every way that I know, surely if there is any blame here it is not to be laid at his poor feet. If either of us is to blame, if either of us has angered You, it must surely have been me.

Then why was I left behind, Lord? Why take Nathan's gift away and not mine? Have you left me here to face even greater horrors, worse sadnesses? Has my punishment only begun?

Well, if this is Your plan, Lord, of course I will abide it. And I praise you now for what I know will be my salvation, my protection, my very survival. And if things go another way, I praise you now through prayer for reuniting me with Nathan in Your loving presence. Until that time, I will go on serving You with faith and love and gratitude for Your blessings for all the days of my life.

Yours in Christ, Mona Mol.

*

The next morning was the second day after Nathan's death, one day before the funeral. The entire community was contributing to the services, as was customary. The Baxters were donating their house, which was close to

21

Resting Hill, where many members of the congregation were buried. The Riley clan were contributing much of the food, being the leading bakers of meat and fruit pies in the area. With the preparations taken care of, Mona had only to marshal her strength and prepare to bury her husband, dead at twenty-one years old.

CHAPTER TWO

Before the funeral there was another long day of quiet contemplation, misery hanging over the household. Stern, stalwart Lucas kept out of it. It had never been his way to discuss emotional matters, and this time in particular he stuck to his traditional duties of labor and leadership and left the more tender aspects of parenting to his wife, Betty.

Mona could sense Betty's attention, and she knew what was inspiring it. There was a bond between daughters which transcended the ages, as vital to Mona and Betty as to any female pair bound by blood and birth. But Mona always felt that there was an unspoken connection between them, a closeness that neither could deny nor ignore, and neither wanted to.

So Mona wasn't surprised when Betty stepped quietly into the kitchen and took her place next to Mona at the table. Mona was shelling peas, tossing the little green morsels into one bowl and the empty pods in the other. Betty picked a few pods out and began shelling the peas herself, the two women working together, side by side, for the first time in years.

"I ... I know these aren't the terms either of us would have chosen," Betty said timidly, words pushing out of her thin lips, "but ... it is nice to have you home, Mona, to have you here like before."

Mona tried to smile, but her minor success was short-lived. Betty went on, "It is terrible though, isn't it? I ... I know there's nothing I can say, no way I can take away the sorrow you're feeling. If I could, if I could somehow take an axe and cut off my hand to restore your contentment —"

"Mamm, stop, don't be silly. You're such a good woman, caring, loving, no girl could have had a better mamm. Don't worry about me, I'll be okay."

Betty tossed another empty pod into the bowl, eyes locked on Mona. "I know you will be soon, but ... in the meantime, you need some help, my daughter, and from those you love most."

This word stopped Mona from working, her fingers freezing around the pod.

Love.

But Mona resisted the temptation to think any further about it. With her mamm ready to talk, she didn't have to. "And what a love you shared, you and your Nathan. Ever since you were children, almost from the day you met, we

24

all knew you'd be married." Betty stared off with a cozy smile, recollections of years past revisiting her imagination. "You two were practically inseparable, along with Gil, of course. Ever since we moved here from Ohio, you three were like Shadroack, Michac and Abendego."

Mona smiled, the same memories called in her own memory. But the famous Hebrew children her mamm mentioned had been put through trials Mona herself knew she would not survive. She could only hope she wouldn't have to find out, but moment by moment Mona could feel that hope slipping away.

"Such a delightful little crew of young ones," Betty said, her head shaking slowly as if in bittersweet disbelief. "How they do grow up quickly."

Mona had heard the old expression before, but as she sat in the kitchen where she'd helped prepare, devour, and then clean up after so many meals, she felt the full weight of the truth behind it. She had grown up quickly, however slow the process seemed at the time. But looking back, Mona realized she'd become a different person than the child who'd lived there all those years; she was no longer the starry-eyed dreamer, but the reasoning woman that time had allowed her the chance to become, the woman God intended her to be. Mona wasn't sure who that woman was,

25

especially in this time of crisis, but she knew who she wasn't; little Mona Tillerman.

Betty sighed. "Well, at least you had that time with Nathan, a chance to experience true love, a love for the ages, eh?" Mona could hardly respond, the words falling into the pit of her soul like jagged rocks, tearing away chunks of her inner being as they tumbled into the darkness. "And a love like that," Betty went on, "that comes to us only once in a generation, or even less."

Mona turned to look at her mamm, Betty Rose Tillerman, with a new and different perspective. Mona could see the lines in her mamm's face, tracing from the corners of her eyes and from her nostrils to the corners of her mouth.

"What about you, Mamm? Is that the kind of love you and Daed share, a love for the ages?"

Betty couldn't help but chuckle, and seemed relieved to be able to do so. "Heavens no, Mona. Your daed and I met and courted and married because it seemed well that we should, and it was well that we did. We did as most people do, which is just as we both grew up anticipating that we would. And you see how splendidly it has worked out, for we have you and Charlie, and perhaps grandchildren later.

There are tragedies in life, Daughter, but there is contentment as well."

"Contentment," Mona repeated, "but not love."

"Oh my little dreamer, haven't you learned by now that what you're thinking of as love is merely … well, it's a kind of vanity."

"Vanity?"

Betty nodded, but her brows arched in sympathy. "The only love you or any of us need worry about is the love of God, and that comes to us by His grace, not by our deeds. The need for adoration from others, or the need to adore others, that puts us above God in our own eyes, Mona. And what greater vanity could there be? 'Love me and I love you,' some say, but where is God in their declaration?"

Mona sat, a cold nausea growing in her belly. She said nothing, unable to fashion a proper thought for all the confused misgivings in her heart and mind. She was nowhere near putting them into words, for fear of what truth they might reveal.

Instead, Betty went on, "Not that you should regret the love you shared with Nathan, as it was a rare and sacred gift, a real blessing." After a pause which was both tender and tart, Betty had to add, "I only hope it won't make saying goodbye to him all the more difficult for you."

27

*

Mona and her brother and parents stood with the grieving Mol couple in the front of the house Nathan and Mona shared, where the first two services would take place. The first would be private, for immediate family only, while the community waited for a larger service to include a sermon for the entire congregation.

Among the sad-faced friends and neighbors to greet Mona and the others was Gillard Durant, his eyes finding Mona's from several yards away, even through the crowd. He wore a sad smile on his handsome, clean-shaven face. He was comforting as he reached his arms out and gave Mona a warm and loving hug. With a pat on the back, he released his grip and turned to the Mols. "I'm so sorry for your loss, Mona. He was a good man, a good friend."

"He held you in a very high regard," Lucas said to Gil, his voice rigid and stern. "In particular your ... artistic inclination."

Gil nodded with an awkward chuckle. "A feeling I know you never shared."

"We all serve God in our own way," Lucas said. "Your ... carvings help to keep the coffers filled, and that does you honor."

"My Aunt Gerta sends her condolences," Gil said. "She wanted to come, but was too weak, I'm afraid. I insisted she stay in bed."

"She's not improving," Mona said.

Gil sighed. "It's the most persistent flu I've ever seen. I fear she may be joining my parents sooner rather than later."

"It's her will to live," Ruth said, her voice cracked with hours of continuous sobbing. She was speaking from new and terrible experience, her words as limp as her tone. "She's lost her desire to go on in this world. She has nothing to live for, why live at all?"

"No more of that talk," Lucas said, "recall our conversation of last evening, Wife. There's to be no further melancholy, I won't allow it!"

Ruth's gaze drifted away, her lips barely managing to fashion an exhausted, "Yes, Husband," in reply.

*

Mona and the Mols joined Deacon Calvin Christoph for a private service. Nathan lay in that pine box, his white suit clean, his face handsome and at peace. Mona looked at that motionless mask, hands folded in front of him, absolutely still then and forever more. But Mona couldn't help but recall the years which had come before, surely the best of

29

their lives. In the stunning clarity of her imagination, Mona was once more just ten years old, meeting young Nathan and his friend Gil for the first time, smiling at their courtesy and kindness and their eager welcome. In the blink of her mind's eye, Mona was twelve and standing in a field of tall grass and daisies, Nathan and Gil holding hickory branches like longswords, fencing with melodramatic flare for her hand. Gil would inevitably take the fall, clearing the way for Mona and Nathan's happy ending.

Deacon Christoph's words rolled in the muffled distance around her, barely piercing the cloak of imagination and memory which consumed her. It was as if she wasn't there at all, not in that sad little study, Ruth once more sobbing in the chair next to her. Mona was not a twenty-year-old widow, but a sweet Amish girl of just sixteen, sweetly holding Nathan's hand during a fall festival hay ride, branches of the cottonwoods drifting slowly by above them. The moon was much higher still, full and bright while the crickets played their haunting lullaby.

But the memories couldn't preserve Mona for long, and her eyes and ears brought her back to the terrible truth. She was not sixteen, she was a twenty-year-old widow, even then looking down at the lifeless corpse of her husband and childhood sweetheart.

Ruth kept sobbing, Lucas unable to console her, and Mona unable to turn a deaf ear. Ruth's pain was overwhelming for her, but it only made Mona feel emptier inside, more nauseous. And as if to willingly distract herself from the creeping truth which was scratching at the back of her brain, Mona focused on the Deacon's words.

"'Ye are of God, little children, and have overcome them: because greater is he that is in you, than he that is in the world. They are of the world: therefore speak they of the world, and the world heareth them. We are of God: he that knoweth God heareth us; he that is not of God heareth not us. Hereby know we the spirit of truth, and the spirit of error. Beloved, let us love one another: for love is of God; and every one that loveth is born of God, and knoweth God.'"

Mona knew why the deacon had chosen that passage, from I John 4. He was reminding her and the grieving Mols that their love for Nathan would endure, it would transcend death, that love survived and would always survive. But he was also saying that love was greater than Nathan or Mona or the Mols, and this only drove a greater and more painful truth deeper into Mona's troubled heart.

"'He that loveth not knoweth not God; for God is love. In this was manifested the love of God toward us, because that God sent his only begotten Son into the world, that we might live through him. Herein is love, not that we loved God, but that he loved us, and sent his Son to be the propitiation for our sins.'"

*

After the community service and a viewing for the county, the coffin was marched up Resting Hill and buried, marked with a plan pine headboard which would soon rot away, like the body beneath it. After that, the hundreds of visitors met at the Baxter house for a feast of meat and fruit pies, casseroles and biscuits, lemonade and cold milk and locally brewed Amish beer. This was a time of fellowship, to remember the dead and to celebrate the living, to remember the past and look forward to the future.

But Mona could take no solace in any of it. She couldn't taste the salty chicken or the buttery, flakey pie crusts, the cool milk as it coated her throat. Nothing had any flavor at all, in fact, something which would have frightened her if Mona's numbness wasn't so overwhelming.

And afterward, when those who had eaten made way for those about to eat, in the gathering crowd behind the

Baxters' big house, Mona could hardly feel the sunlight upon her face, her ears unable to find the songs of the yellow warblers and the tan chickadees hiding in the cedar branches around her. Mona and her mamm Betty were making their way toward Gil and Lucas and the other men when they were approached by two young men, the beefy Roland brothers, Peter and Paul. With grim faces and black hats in their hands, they approached sheepishly, big shoulders lurching up toward their big, splayed ears.

"Sister Mol," Peter said to them, "we're just so sorry about what happened."

"Our buggy wheel broke, as you know," Paul added. "We couldn't call. If only Nathan had waited for us."

But Peter snapped at his brother, "You lay blame at a dead man's feet at his own funeral, to his widowed wife? You numbskull!"

"Boys, please," Mona said, "it's all right, thank you for your kind words. Nathan spoke of you often, he was quite pleased to have been working with you." The brothers nodded, glanced at one another, then backed away to let Mona and Betty join the rest of their family.

Mona took her place under a pignut hickory with Liv and her husband Ross, who held their one-year-old daughter Jesse in his arms. But his steely attention was

33

fixed on Mona. Everybody could see how troubled Mona was, how the horrific and sudden nature of Nathan's death had stunned her. In a private consultation, the deacon had said she was shocked, the same way many war veterans are by the horrors of combat. Her own mamm Betty suggested Mona felt guilty for surviving her young husband, irrational though it may have been. But Ross Schmidt didn't seem convinced of either theory. And as he looked at Mona with his unflinching blue eyes, piercing hers like to knitting needles which dug right into the center of her brain, it was as if Ross could read her mind. It was as if Ross knew what Mona was thinking and feeling even more than she did.

But she was fast coming to learn the secrets of her own heart, no longer able to avoid or ignore them.

Can it be, Mona had to ask herself in her quiet conscience, *that this hollowness inside me isn't shock or mourning but simply ... nothing, an empty space where shock or grief should be but isn't? Is it possible that God is now forcing me to ask myself the one question I've always considered answered, a question that didn't need to be asked?*

Did I really love Nathan at all?

Of course I had love for him, Mona could reassure herself, *he was an old and dear friend. And I know as I*

34

child I harbored a child's crush, and there was simply
nothing to ever challenge or change that. Just as Liv said,
everybody assumed we'd be married, ourselves first and
foremost. But ... is that why we married, simply because we
assumed that we would, simply because it seemed a
foregone conclusion with nothing to stand in its way?

Mona's gut turned to a hot soup, bile bubbling over and
crawling up the back of her throat.

Can it be as my mamm described, that all love is simply
a matter of resolve and acceptance, that anything else is
simple folly? Are we really creatures of love only for God,
and for each other we are merely ... tolerant? Is that the
love St. Paul speaks of, and St. Peter, and even King Jesus
himself? No, such love cannot be merely vanity, as my
Mamm suggests, it must be more than just a flight of fancy!
I can hear it in the terrible wail of the grief-stricken Ruth
Mol. I can see it in the eyes of my friend Liv when she looks
into Ross' eyes and he back into hers. I know love is real,
and that it travels among us, the merely human. It was a
love I thought I shared with Nathan, and never wanted to
lie to him or be anything other than a good Amish wife and
mamm to his children, but ...

Mona tried not to think about it, struggling to distract herself from the terrible conclusion she could already see coming.

... But I see now that what Nathan and I had, it may have been love, but it wasn't ... I wasn't in love with him? Can it be?

But Mona didn't have to go on asking herself, as she'd already found the answer in the echoing silence of her soul, a quick cold coming over her, chills running the length of her body and collecting in her skull, shaking it with enough force to throw her into a convulsion, the darkness returning to overtake her.

*

Mona woke up under the same pignut tree, her family and friends gathered around her. They wore sad and confused expressions, eyebrows arched and mouths in puckered, little frowns.

Mona tried to lift her head, and she looked up to see her daed Lucas's head above hers, his lap supporting her. He eased her back down and said, "Take it easy, child, an ambulance is on the way."

"Another trip to the Englischer hospital," Mona said, "they don't do anything and they know even less." Mona turned to see the old face of Ulga Frau looking down at her with a wry little smile on her wrinkled, slightly whiskered face. The congregation's midwife, her presence brought instant alarm to Mona's confused conscience. "Ulga Frau," she said, "why do I need an ambulance? Am I dying?"

"Not at all, child," Ulga said in a deep, aging voice, "you're pregnant."

CHAPTER THREE

Mona did go back to Adams County General, where they confirmed her pregnancy. "It explains a lot," Dr. Larson said, "from your little spells to your other, more severe blackouts. Low blood sugar, hormones —"

"Shouldn't this have come up in the tests you ran?"

"Results could have gotten lost."

"Lost?"

Doctor Larson glanced around the little examination room. "Let me tell you something, Mona. You may think we're a bunch of magicians with racks of powerful medicines and computers, superheroes in white coats. But this is a hospital, Mona, bad things happen here. Accidents, switched charts, spoiled blood samples. This is the emergency room, and I'm one of the only doctors you'll find here at any given time. I go from drug overdoses to slash wounds, sometime for sixteen hours at a stretch and I'm not the only one. We do our best, but still ..."

Pregnant. Could that be why I'm feeling so strangely, Mona wondered, *as it regards my feelings for Nathan? Hormones change your moods, the doctor just said so.*

Mona wasn't entirely convinced, but she also knew that it hardly mattered. Nathan was dead, and she was carrying his child. The unborn life was more important than the life which had passed, however misunderstood that life may have been.

And once back at the Tillerman home, Lucas paced the living room while Mona sat on the couch, her mamm Betty sitting with her arms wrapped around Mona's shoulders. Charlie sat respectfully.

Betty said, "I know this is … unexpected, but surely it's a blessing."

Lucas said, "One which must be dealt with, and in the good and proper manner."

Mona said, "Well, of course I'm going to have the child."

"Of course," Lucas snapped back, "you'd suggest otherwise, in front of your kid sister?"

Betty said, "Please, Husband, your tone — "

"My tone is the least of our worries," Lucas said. "The child needs a father, and the sooner the better!"

"Husband, no," Betty said, "we can't just marry our daughter off, her poor husband's body isn't even cold in the ground."

"Please don't speak of me as if I weren't sitting right here," Mona said.

"Then tell us," Lucas said, "what would you do?" Mona searched her mind and heart, but found no answer. So Lucas went on to Betty, "See what I mean? We'll have to make the choices here ... or *I* will."

"She can come back here to live with us again," Betty said, "a happy family once more. We'll raise the child together! I would cherish the opportunity to raise another — "

"No," Mona said, "the child is mine to raise, my responsibility."

"One you cannot fulfill alone," Lucas said. "Don't feel slighted or angry, my child."

"I'm *not* a child."

"That's right, Daughter, you're *with* child. And you'd better start thinking in those terms ... and acting likewise!" After a long and heaving silence, Lucas said, "We'll find a husband and daed for the child and that's that," before stepping slowly out of the room.

*

The next day Mona went to visit Liv. Gil's carved grizzly bear stood out front while Ross worked in the fields in the back, Mona trying to relax with a cup of hot Amish tea while little Jesse played on the living room floor.

"Don't worry," Liv said, "I'm sure everything will work out. God is always in control."

"I know that, Liv, of course. But where God is leading me, and whether I have the courage to follow, *that* I do *not* know."

"Of course you do, Mona, but … you'll have to gather that courage now. Your daed is determined?" Mona nodded, and Liv went on, "He's not known for his patience, is he?" They both giggled, but there was no mirth in it. Liv said, "I don't mean to beat a … to repeat myself, Mona, but … what about Gil?"

Even though she already knew the answer, Mona couldn't help but ask, "What about Gil?"

"For a husband, I mean. Mona, he already loves you, everybody knows it — "

"Stop saying that, Liv, nobody knows any such thing! Who have you been talking to, and about me, no less?"

Liv shrugged. "It's been years, Liv, and he never married?"

"He's an artist — "

"He's in love with you, Mona, and no other woman has measured up, it's as simple as that."

"That's not true, Liv. First of all, he's married to his work. He's so focused on it, when he's working it's as if he's in another world. And he is exceptional at it, isn't he?" Mona felt herself drifting off, a little smile digging its way into her left cheek. "And there's his aunt to see to — "

"Don't you think if he got married it might give his aunt hope, a reason to carry on, something worth living for?"

"A family — you think that would make a difference?"

"Of course I do. You heard your mother-in-law, Gerta's lost her will to live. But look at what her family has faced; Gil's mother died in childbirth, his father just a decade later. Then his good and dutiful aunt and uncle step in to raise the boy. Two years in, the uncle dies. Now the aunt has to look around see that her past has died away and her future is empty, it doesn't even exit. No grandniece or grandnephew, no love for her sole surviving family member, who toils night and day on lifeless sculptures carved out of dead tree trunks."

Mona understood the way Liv was seeing things, and she couldn't disagree. "Gil should find a nice girl," Mona said, "I've always encouraged him to do that. But I can't be that girl, not … now, not anymore."

Liv leaned forward, setting a hand on Mona's leg. "How do you mean, *anymore*?"

"We friends now," Mona said, "such good friends now that ... I don't think we could become anything else. Maybe ... maybe before, years ago, but I ... I didn't make that choice — "

"We don't choose love," Liv said, "love chooses us."

"No, no, you don't understand."

"You're right, Mona, I don't understand; help me to understand, explain it to me!"

"Because we're such close friends now, Liv, what if that changes? What if it's a misguided notion and it destroys our friendship? I don't think I could survive that, not now. And I don't think Gil wants to lose another friendship either. He was almost as close to Nathan as I was."

"And there's always the matter of appearances," Liv said, "always close to Gil's heart."

"But he's right. You know how people can be, especially in towns like ours; people gossip, make assumptions, their sympathy turns to acid scrutiny. And those are barbs I'm likely to face enough as it is. If anything, I need Gil's protection from that, not to let him be the cause of even greater troubles. And it could be worse for him, destroy his reputation, render his works entirely without value."

Liv looked deep into Mona's eyes. "You wouldn't put money over love?"

"No, never. But I … I just don't think it's what God intends for either of us, or … or surely things would have gone differently, surely they would have."

A long silence passed between them, Mona needing to say nothing more. So Liv answered merely, "They yet may."

*

Two weeks passed into three, Mona and her family trying to recover some normalcy in their lives. The Tillermans decided that Mona should stay in the family home during her pregnancy and allowed a visiting Amish family from Lancaster County in Pennsylvania to stay there and keep the family bee hives and vegetable gardens.

Mona helped her mother around the house and saw Charlie to and from school, and she gave long and fruitless hours to considering her future.

And Mona apparently wasn't the only one.

Mona began noticing the looks she was attracting from her friends and neighbors. When Nathan died, she'd been treated to a parade of sympathetic expressions, foreheads furrowed and mouths downturned in caring little pouts. But once the news of her pregnancy got around, those frowns became a bit wider, the brows more furrowed but not arching upward in empathy, but downward in disdain.

Mona had never welcomed their sorrow or pity, and she certainly could not feel comfortable shouldering the brunt of their contempt. The more aware of it she became, the more confused by it she was.

What do they think of me, Mona wondered, *that I carry the devil's own seed in my belly?*

Mona said nothing of it to anyone, but on a third Sunday when she and her family were resoundingly ignored by the others at services, Mona felt it prudent to take a private meeting with Deacon Christoph in the hours of fellowship after the meal.

Strolling around the side yard of the Douglass family home, whose turn it was to host the massive congregation, Deacon Christoph glanced at a passing cardinal, fluttering by in a blur of red and black.

"I wouldn't over-worry about them," the deacon said, his thinning brown hair clinging to the sides of his head like a graying donut. "Though I confess they might be … anxious about your condition, and your position."

"No more so than I, Deacon, I can assure you."

"And, if I may ask, what conclusions have you drawn about your ... immediate future?"

Mona sighed, an answer still eluding her. But she knew one thing: "I've concluded that it's my own future, and very much my own concern. What would they have me do?"

Deacon Christoph shrugged. "As you say, it is your future. Different people would have different expectations, no two precisely the same. But whatever you do, child, know that it has already been a month since Nathan's passing. Your pregnancy, like time itself, marches forward."

*

Mona went straight to Liv, whom she knew would give her an honest report. "Well, there have been rumblings," Liv said, "not that I take any part in them. But one does hear things, especially in a town this small."

"And what things are one hearing?"

"Just that, well, that you're raising the child ... out of wedlock."

"Liv, I'm a widow! It wasn't my choice!"

"No, Mona, of course not." Little Jesse wriggled in her mamm's grip. "But you do have a choice now."

"To find a man?" Liv didn't need to answer, turning her attention to Jesse before the toddler finally escaped her loving clutches and began stumbling around the room. "It just doesn't feel right."

"I know, Mona, I really do."

"No, you don't," Mona found her self saying, too fast to stop herself. "How could you? Your husband is alive, you don't know what it's like to be in this situation."

After a guilty pause, Liv could only nod. "You're right, Mona, and I'm sorry for your loss."

"It's not just that, Liv, but … " There were things Mona still couldn't put into words, confessions she wasn't ready to share with her best friend or anybody else; secrets she was ready to take to her own grave. "I think about Nathan, and … I … I wonder if he wouldn't be … hurt or offended or dishonored — "

"No, Mona, you're looking at it all wrong. You're right, you didn't choose this, and Nathan didn't either. If he could have survived that accident to raise his own child, of course he would have. But now you have a different set of choices. And don't you think he would want his son to be raised by a good and decent man? Don't you think he would want you to spend the rest of your days on Earth in some contentment?"

"Contentment," Mona repeated, "is that the best I can hope for?"

"It's the best any of us can hope for," Liv said. "I know it's not your ideal, but ... what choice do you really have?"

"My child would still have my mamm and daed. My mamm's champing at the bit to raise another little one. Perhaps that's not such a bad idea. My daed could be as good and strong an example than some man I find on the street, I know Nathan wouldn't want that."

"Not just some man from off the street," Liv repeated with disgust. "There are lots of good men out there, some a lot closer than you think."

"Not Gil again, Liv — "

"No, Mona, you've made yourself clear about Gil. But ... there are others, and lots of them. We're in Adams County, it's one of the biggest Amish populations in the country, Mona. Ross knows several possible candidates — "

"Candidates? Oh Lord, it sounds like Englischer politics! We can all see the results of that grim process!"

But Liv laughed it off. "You just let me take care of everything."

Mona bit her lower lip, eyes rolling nervously. "I don't know, Liv — "

"Mona, I'm your best friend, I wouldn't steer you wrong."

"No, of course not, Liv."

With another little chuckle, Liv added, "And if I don't step in, that'll leave it to your daed. And how do you imagine that's going to turn out?"

"I don't even want to think about it." The two friends shared a laugh, and it felt good.

*

Mona had been keeping up her visits to the Mol couple. As the weeks went on, Ruth's grieving seemed finally to subside. When she came it only seemed to upset Ruth even more, and Mona had to question the value of continuing her visits. But finally Mona seemed to be bringing the Mols more comfort than misery, and she was glad she'd followed her instincts and not abandoned them. Poor William and Ruth had lost their one and only son, and now they were facing the prospect of losing not only their daughter-in-law, but their only grandchild as well.

"It really is good of you to come and see us, Mona," Ruth said, her smile weary and careworn.

"We are still family," Mona said.

"You truly feel that way," William said, as much a question as a statement. Mona nodded, and Lucas added,

"We can only hope now that we never treated you with less than a proper welcome."

"No," Mona said, only slightly confused.

"We were always so glad that God brought you and our Nathan together," Ruth said. "If I was a bit protective, or he a bit stern, it was only for love of our only child."

"Of course," Mona answered, "I never would have thought anything else. But you needn't have worried, I've always thought of you both as friends, even closer than that."

William and Ruth exchanged a knowing glance, then returned their attention to Mona. "We're very glad to hear you say that, Mona, and you should know we've always felt the same about you."

Mona nodded. "I'm glad. You'll both always be welcome to visit with the child, of course, just as family should. There won't be a single gathering or celebration without you both being present." An awkward tension passed before the Mols shared one more look.

William said to Mona, "We understand that you are weighing your choices for the future."

Mona's muscles tightened around her neck and shoulders. "I am."

William went on, "And as the child's grandparents, you can imagine that we have a keen interest as to what that future might include."

Mona did, and was about to say so, but Ruth didn't give her the chance. "We only want what's best for the child, of course."

This was what Mona wanted too, but didn't feel the need to say so. And William didn't give her time: "My wife and I strongly feel that you are not in an idea situation to raise the child."

"I am considering finding a proper man to be the child's daed."

"There is only one proper man for that position," William said, "and he is now in the company of our Creator. We do not wish for our grandchild to be raised by some stranger, chosen almost at random by a girl unfairly pressured from all sides."

"So you'd pressure me from your own side before the others can begin their assault?"

Ruth repeated, "Assault? Such language!"

"I'm sorry for the manner," Mona said, "but not the matter. I will be the child's mamm, and there could be no person more qualified to be the parent."

"Then you may join us here if you like."

Mona sat in stunned silence, disbelief making it a challenge to digest what they were suggesting. "Join you here?"

"Of course," Ruth said, "as you said, we're all family."

"But … no, I'm afraid … no."

After a cold silence, William said, "We're told you've considered raising the child without a daed in your parents' home. Is there some way in which we are less able to raise the child than they?"

"Well, no," Mona said, "that's not what I mean to say at all."

"Then what *do* you mean to say," William asked. "That we are altogether too unpleasant for your company? That we're unworthy to raise the child?"

"No, neither of those things."

"Then do what is right," William said, his voice low and quick and strong. "Give us the child to raise on our own, participate however much or little your conscience will allow."

Ruth's voice began to crack again. "Look into your heart, child, and know that this is surely what God intends."

Mona stood up, her head shaking slightly. "No, I don't believe that it is," she said, stepping backward toward the door. "I know you're both still hurting from Nathan's loss, and that you think you've found some way to hold onto him, to go on raising him as your child forever. But this isn't Nathan growing in my womb, but a new and different life; this is my child, not yours. How can you presume to — ?""

"We make no presumptions," William said, a loud snap to his voice. "You are the one ready to sacrifice the child's wellbeing for your own selfish and I dare say childish ends!"

"You'd take my child from out of my very womb and then call me selfish?"

"You're not thinking straight," Ruth said. "Please just give it some reflection, you'll see for yourself that it's best for the child."

"It's best for *you*," Mona said, opening the door and backing out of the house with greater urgency, a growing fear curling in the back of her brain. "But you won't take my child, you hear me? You won't, you won't!"

With that, Mona staggered out of the house and down the porch steps. She climbed up on the buggy as William and Ruth arrived at the front door, watching her with impassive expressions, unfazed and undeterred. Mona shook the reins and tried to ignore the Mols as the

Tillerman mare Clip-Clop pulled her forward and then away from the Mol house.

She vowed never to return.

*

Lucas hardly touched his dinner, a plate of smothered pork chops, applesauce, mashed potatoes and hot peas slathered in butter. But he was blind to it; blind with rage. "That William Mol, how could he devise such a plan? He's no better than Lilith herself, snatching children out of the cradle!"

With a glance at young Charlie, Betty said to Lucas, "Husband, please."

A brief silence returned to the dinner table, Mona and Betty sharing a worried glance. Lucas tried to resume in a calmer tone. "That fellow was always an aggressor, thrusting you two together even as children."

Mona looked up from her plate, unable to stop herself from saying, "No, Daed, no."

"What's that?"

"No," Mona went on, "you … you both wanted us to marry, you all did."

"It was never our choice," Betty said. "You fell in love, we were supportive as good parents should be."

"When the young man is worthy," Lucas added, "and Nathan was. Funny I never gave his parents the same scrutiny."

Mona asked, "You scrutinized Nathan?"

"Of course," Lucas was quick to say. "What good daed wouldn't?"

"Then is Mr. Mol really so wrong to scrutinize me?" Mona's logic had her daed stumped.

After a bite of his mashed potatoes, dripping in brown gravy, Lucas said, "You're the child's mother and your place is together. If you're not to share your lives with a man to be husband and daed, then at the very least you belong here with your own natural parents, and not with veritable strangers."

Betty said, "Have sympathy, Husband. They're suffering."

"Then they're in no position to raise a child!"

All eyes fell upon Mona, the unspoken question echoing in every ear, resting on every stilled tongue. Until Charlie, in all her innocence, said, "Are you suffering, Mona?"

Once asked, the answer became more and more clear. But while Mona was getting closer to admitting it, she didn't dare do so to her kid sister. Instead, Betty said to the boy, "She is, in a different sort of way."

Lucas added, "Your sister has put aside her own grief in order to face the greater matter of your future niece or nephew's wellbeing. You'd be well to remember it when trials of your own come to pass."

Another long, tense silence passed. Lucas shook his head and opened another Amish beer. "And at such a time, when we're all so emotionally vulnerable and highly strung?"

"It is a bit unseemly," Betty said.

Lucas repeated, "Unseemly? It's unheard of! How should they raise the child before us? As if they were better than we?"

Mona had to point out, "They said the same thing about you two."

Lucas asked her, "And what's that supposed to mean?"

"It means you're both treating my unborn child as if it were some prize to be fought over by rabid dogs!"

"Daughter!"

"No, Daed, I won't have it. How can you all presume to raise my child? I knew it was a mistake to come back into this house."

Lucas's voice got louder and angrier, little Charlie shrinking down in her wooden chair. "In this house or in this state or any other, you're still our family, Mona, and you always will be. Your child no less so."

"No less family," Mona said, "but this child is mine to raise, no less than I was yours."

"*Was*," Betty sadly repeated.

Mona glanced at Charlie. "You still have Charlie to raise."

Charlie rolled her eyes and shook her head to comedic effect. "Maybe *I* should be the one to get married!" The family shared a relieved chuckle, but it didn't last.

*

Mona took the family horse and buggy into the little shopping district just a few miles from her family home. She met the first of her suitors on the bench under the old sugarberry tree in the northwest corner of President Benjamin Harrison Park. It was very close to a carved statue, jagged lines from the chainsaw giving the depiction of an upraised hand and arm a handsome texture. It was one of Gil's creations, commissioned by the city government and granted to him in a statewide competition. The tree was a dead green ash and had been growing in that spot, chosen as the subject and turned over to Gil to design and then

57

render his creation. He called it *Another Adam* and its outstretched fingers resembled a famous painting Mona only vaguely knew, the hand of mankind reaching up while the Hand of God reached down.

I'll have to ask Gil about that, Mona noted, *the original piece he was inspired by.* But not wanting to be rude, Mona turned her attention back to Albert Gretchinson, sitting on the bench next to her. He'd held his rigid silence for ten minutes, ever since he approached and sat down next to him.

She said, "So you're a friend of Ross. He's a good man." Albert slowly turned to look at her, then nodded. Mona tried to smile, but it wasn't easy. "I'm grateful to him for arranging this … this introduction." Another long stretch of complete silence followed.

Mona cleared her throat and went on, "You've heard of my … unfortunate set of circumstances?" Albert just nodded, eyes still on the park around them. "It's very … open-minded and kindhearted of you to welcome me as you're doing."

There was no response from the stern, rigid young man, his bony face missing the customary marital beard. And the reason for that absence was uppermost on Mona's mind. "I'm afraid you have me at a bit at a disadvantage," she said with a hopeful little smile. "You know how it is that I've come here, but I know almost nothing of you."

Albert turned his head very slowly, his gaze finally finding Mona's. "You're quite free with your tongue."

A stunned pause clung to the air before Mona asked even though she'd heard quite clearly, "I beg your pardon?"

Slower, with greater clarity, Albert said, "You speak too much for a woman."

"Now you look here — "

"'But I say unto you, That every idle word that men shall speak, they shall give account thereof in the day of judgment.'"

Mona leaned back a bit. "Don't you presume to throw Matthew up at me!"

"Ecclesiastes, then: 'The beginning of the words of his mouth is foolishness: and the end of his talk is mischievous madness.'"

"10:13."

"Very good," Albert said. "You may yet be a worthy woman."

"A worth you'll never measure," Mona said, already on her feet. "What kind of happiness, or even contentment, can you offer with such a rigid disposition?"

"That of everlasting blessings in the presence of the Lord."

"You think that's the only way to His heart? He gave us the capacity for joy, don't you think He wants us to exercise that capacity?"

"No, I most certainly do not," Albert said. "Don't you see my Amish plains, or your own? Our way is to refuse such ... contentment, until we find it with the Lord."

"No sir, I don't see it that way at all. We're meant to resist certain temptations, that's true. But we're meant to find love and contentment and even joy, yes even that! So long as we find joy in the proper things, the things God gives us to enjoy. And love is one of those things."

Mona walked away, not wishing to be rude but not willing to spend another moment in that cold man's company.

*

Mona was quick to return to Liv and Ross' to explain what had happened with Ross' friend Albert. "I didn't mean to be rude," Mona said, fingers fidgeting with the handle of her little tea cup. "But he was just so ... so cold and rigid."

"You could hardly have a more reliable or stalwart Amish man to raise your child in the Old Order fashion."

"I don't doubt that he would be reliable," Mona said. "But I don't think I would want to rely on a steady stream of *that*."

Liv said to Ross, "Why would you choose him of all people? You know Mona needs a more … easygoing type of man."

"Nathan was hardly easygoing. Hardworking, quite stern actually. Sure, he used to play around when he was a kid, like all kids do. But he grew up, as most of us manage."

Mona asked, "How do you mean that?"

Pausing to choose his words, Ross said, "Take your friend Gil, for example. Good friend, and that's just fine. I like Gil — "

"You have one of his carvings in your front yard," Mona reminded him.

"And it's quite a handsome piece. But … to be an artist? To spend his manly years playing in the mud?"

"God blessed him with gifts," Mona said. "And they don't include playing in the mud! He uses a chainsaw to do those carvings, it's very dangerous!"

"Exactly," Ross said. "I'd even call it reckless and foolish! Meanwhile he has no wife, no child, he cannot even care for his poor aunt. She wastes away … "

61

"He's tending to her the best he can," Mona said, "he makes sacrifices for her, and for his art. Why are you in such a bitter temper over Gil?"

"I'm not, Mona, honestly. But your friend ... *our* friend ... is an example, to you and to us all. Is *that* the kind of man you would want to raise your child?"

*

With all the talk of Gil, Mona decided to take an afternoon to pay a visit to her old friend. She could hear the chainsaw buzzing even before she reached the edge of the long gravel driveway. And as Clip-Clop drew her nearer, Mona felt a pang of excitement and curiosity shoot through her. She delighted in asking herself, *What's he creating this time? What's his divine inspiration is whispering in his ear today?*

Mona climbed down off the buggy with a picnic basket she'd brought, walked around the side of the house. While she normally would never think to be so presumptuous, she'd been such good friends with Gil for so long, there was no need for the formality of knocking on the front door. He was working in the back, he couldn't have heard it anyway, and she'd only risk disturbing Aunt Gerta.

As Mona walked around to the backyard, her eyes on the concrete slab which was the center of the yard. Gil and

Nathan had poured the foundation themselves, an ideal workplace for Gil's heavy tree trunks, the canvases he used to create his masterpieces during the sunny spring and summer months.

Mona was struck by the beauty of the carving standing on that slab, only half-finished as Gil drew his roaring chainsaw over its surface. Clouds of wood dust wafted around him, peering through his safety goggles at his developing creation. The gas fumes from the chainsaw's engine were thick in the air, the noise almost deafening as Mona silently approached.

CHAPTER FOUR

The carving was still very rough, but Mona could already envision the final result. The oak tree trunk was round at the flat-cut bottom, bark still around the edges. As the wood rose, the carving had begun, and the body of the piece itself was no longer solid and thick. It had already been carved into, around and even through. Numerous empty spaces had been carved into the trunk, giving the heavy piece an airy feeling. The wood which remained was carved into bird-like shapes, each connected to another. It was a flock of swallows flying through the air, and it seemed like an impossible feat for such massive tools.

Mona stood in silent respect, not wanting to disturb Gil or, worse, cause him to slip and ruin his carving. Finally Gil stepped back and turned, the engine of the chainsaw idling lower, not so loud.

Gil shut the chainsaw down and took off his goggles. "Mona, what a pleasant surprise."

Mona raised the basket a bit. "I brought some potato soup, for your aunt. How is she?"

Gil only shrugged. "It's very kind of you."

"Not at all." Mona looked the statue over. "Swallows, they were Nathan's favorite."

"They're in his honor. Do you remember how he used to like to watch them, sweeping across the sky, all moving in one direction then another."

Mona nodded, her gaze drifting off to a bittersweet memory. "He used to say it was like a giant hand waving at us from above, like the Hand of God." Mona's heart swelled with warmth, a glow in her soul. "That's very sweet, Gil."

"It's little enough to mark his memory," Gil said, looking the carving over. "S'gonna take a good deal more work. But at least I'm still here to do it."

They shared a sad, tense silence before Gil said, "Why don't you take that soup up to my aunt. I'm sure she'll be thrilled to see you."

*

It made Mona's heart sink to see Gerta Frieling laying in that bed, her blonde hair spread out on the pillow beneath her head. She was very thin beneath those white cotton sheets, her skin almost as pale. She was looking at the doorway, a meek smile stretching tiredly across her wrinkling face.

"Mona," she said, her voice low and grainy, "how lovely to see you again."

Mona tried to smile as she crossed the little bedroom, a hot bowl of the cream of potato soup in her hands. "I brought you some soup, just warmed it up downstairs."

Gerta smiled, but waved it off. "I can't eat. But come and sit with me a bit." Mona approached and pulled up the little chair near the desk and sat by the bedside. "How lovely you are, such a fine young woman. I'm so sorry to hear about your poor Nathan, such a sorrowful turn."

Mona nodded. "It was … tragic."

"No, no," Gerta said with sudden urgency.

"Aunt Gerta?"

"It was sorrowful, for the loss of a good man, leaving you in the family way … without a proper family. It is sad for now, but not tragic, not now or ever." Reading Mona's respectfully silent confusion, "God is in control, child. 'But now hath God set the members every one of them in the body, as it hath pleased him.' God is setting things as He wants them to be, and for some of us, that means to be set aside."

"Aunt Gerta, no — "

"It's so, child. I'll be with the Lord soon enough, and it is well that I should be. I've done my part, to raise Gil when my own dear sister and brother-in-law and husband were called away, one by one. And now my own purpose has passed."

"How can you think such a thing, Aunt Gerta? Gil loves you, he adores you — "

"And so he must be set free of me. And when I go, darling Mona, remember that it is God's will that I go, for me as for any of us. And that when we do go, we go for a reason, a purpose … His purpose."

Mona sat in a stillness she could neither escape nor ignore. "Whatever could that be?"

Gerta reached out, setting her already bony hand on Mona's arm. "That is what we must pray for the wisdom to realize … before it's too late." Gerta looked up with a trembling desperation, as much as her withering body could tolerate. Mona couldn't help but recall how strong and vital Gerta had been when she first came to Adams County, capable and robust. Now she was fading fast, sinking into her bed as if it were her grave. For Gerta, it did seem to be too late. And Mona could see herself in that bed, her own face on Gerta's frail body, her last meaningful thoughts lost on the deaf ears of some young girl, unable to understand what seemed obvious enough.

Mona did understand, and Gerta seemed to realize it. But neither dared to say the words and for the same reason; for fear of scaring Mona away from her true destiny.

*

Mona wasn't home for much longer than a few minutes before she went back to her chores. There was sweeping to be done, and Mona couldn't help but reflect on the day she heard the news about Nathan, how she clung to that broom handle with no hope of it holding her up.

And Mona had to admit that, in the month which had passed, she was every bit as confused and frightened.

"Mona," Lucas said as he stepped into the room.

Mona paused, but then went on sweeping. "Daed."

Lucas crossed toward her. "How are things with you, Daughter? Are you … feeling well?"

"Very," Mona said, "allowing for a bit of worry here and there."

"Despite our faith, fear is everyone's portion." Mona nodded. Her daed was often very stern and withholding of his affection, but he seemed warmer and more comforting now. Mona didn't have to wonder too long or too hard about his change of disposition.

"And how does it go with your … social endeavors?"

Mona knew what he meant, and what he was delicately trying not to say. She answered with, "I'm meeting another young man in just a day or so, another friend of Ross'."

"I see." A long, heavy silence passed. "I hope your efforts bare some fruit, Mona — "

"Before *I* do, is that what you mean to say?"

"You will watch your tone of voice, child!"

"I am *not* a child! I'll be a mamm to my own child soon enough!"

Lucas took a step closer to her. "And this is precisely my point. You have asserted your strength of will, and so far I have abided it. And I will allow you this ... this independence you seek, this authority — "

"Over my own life? Yes!"

"But I will not remain patient for long! If you do not find a suitable daed for your unborn child, if you cannot come to some reasonable choice, then I will have to intervene."

After a moment of disbelief, Mona could only say, "Daed — ?"

"Let us face the facts; you are not proving capable or worthy of making this choice for yourself. It's through no blame of your own, but it seems clear enough. But I do not share your confusion, and my choice will be a sound one, I assure you. Furthermore, you will abide it."

"No, Daed, no — please, I — "

"I have no wish to make you suffer, Mona! You're my daughter and I love you. And that is why I must do whatever I can to ensure your future contentment and that of my grandchild. It is my right and my responsibility to do so, whatever the cost, even if that is your affection. Love me or like me or don't, but I must do what is right." After a sharp silence, he added, "And I will."

*

Stan Larz did not share the usual Amish man's build. Childhoods of farming and rugged play, fed by foods rich in protein and necessary fats, created young men of great strength and robust good health. Even Gil, who was an artist among laborers, had strong arms from lifting those chainsaws for hours on end, hoisting tree trunks and stumps and other heavy gear. But this Stan was flabby and pale, a double-chin rippling with every word.

"You know what they say," he said with a broad smile on his round face, "never trust a thin baker!" He laughed, and Mona offered up a little chuckle. She met him at a little table in front of his own bakery, and she couldn't deny that the man was doing well for himself and for his community.

"I don't mind your weight," Mona said. "I always felt you fell in love with a person, not a body."

"Then we should get along just fine!" They shared a little chuckle. "And I suppose I should be completely honest with you from the very start … "

Once again, Mona felt as if she was being pulled in two different directions. She was glad to hear that he'd be so forthright and respectful of her intelligence. But in Mona's experience, no good sentiment was ever introduced with a phrase like, *I should be completely honest with you ...*

"The truth of it is that … I can't have children of my own. That's why I don't yet have a wife." Glancing down at his round belly, Stan shrugged. "Not the only reason, I suppose. But not all girls are as deep-thinking as you are. The main thing is that, without a family, what is Amish life? What Amish girl would throw away her birthright like that to be with an impotent fat man?"

Mona fumbled for an answer. "Well, I — "

"And here you are," Stan went on, "with a child and no husband. Could it be more clear what God has in mind?"

"I admit, it does seem … convenient."

"More than that," Stan said.

"Let's not … get ahead of ourselves. We've both waited this long just to become introduced, after all — "

"That's my point in a nutshell," Stan interrupted. "We've waited long enough, too long as far as I'm concerned."

"Mister Larz, we've only just met."

"True, true. But that little clock in your belly keeps ticking, eh?" Mona glanced down at her belly, instinctively covering it with one hand. Stan went on, "Look, I know what kind of man your … all I'm saying is, things have changed. It's time."

"It's … it's time?"

"Yes. It's time to settle, Mona."

"Missus Mol," Mona said.

"As you wish. But I think you'll find, Mrs. Mol, that your position is just not as strong as it might have been. Reconsider the breadth of your options, my dear — "

"I'm not your dear," Mona said, "and I never will be."

"You really think you're so special? You're a pregnant widow, Mrs. *Mauled,* you're damaged goods! And if you don't now that by now, you'll discover it soon enough."

"I don't know it! I'm carrying a child, a life, and that's a blessing. I'm a child of the most high God! Damaged goods? How dare you?"

"I didn't mean to be rude. But people like us, we have to accept things the way they are — "

"You may have to," Mona said, turning for another abrupt exit. "I, for one, refuse!"

*

It was only two days later that Mona and the Tillerman family received a visit from William and Ruth Mol. They brought a considerable tension with them, but it was hard to notice the increase with the already rising ire that surrounded the house.

Once settled in the living room around a tray of Amish friendship cookies and herb tea, Ruth said to Mona, "We're so sorry for upsetting you before, Mona. We hadn't thought about how difficult your position already was, so many things to think about and worry over."

"Your own plates were quite full too," Mona said, earning her own mamm's proud smile.

Ruth went on, "We've had time to calm down and reconsider things. We realize how much an affront it must have been, to think we'd take your child from you."

William added, "And we know that, to raise the child in our home, would be neither pleasant nor appropriate for you."

Mona said, "I would never say unpleasant — "

"And if you wish to raise the child here," William went on, "in the house where you yourself were raised, we would raise no objection."

Lucas's posture straightened with this remark. "So much the better for our good nights' rest." Mona suppressed her smile, even turning away to hide it.

But William went on, "We hear that you're out looking for a husband."

"Not for herself," Betty said, "but to find a daed for our grandchild."

"The reason is obvious," William said, his voice level and unforgiving. "As plain to see as the act itself. The whole congregation is talking about it."

Despite herself, Mona asked, "And just what are they saying?"

"That you're skulking the streets in desperation," William said, "sullying your family name and ours, being rejected by those who are already the outcasts of the community."

Mona was stumped, stymied, unable to answer.

Ruth said, "We know you have good intentions, dear, but the way you're going about it, it's just not seemly."

"Not seemly," Lucas repeated. "But for her to raise the child without a proper husband and provider, without a daed of the child's own, that would be more acceptable to you and our gossiping neighbors?"

Ruth was quick to say, "We suggest that you allow us to introduce Mona to some nice young men."

"You?" Lucas shook his head. "I should hardly think."

William snapped back, "And why is that? Can you tell me you're not inclined to do the same thing?"

"Your designs on the child are already well known to us," Lucas said.

William repeated, "Designs? What are you saying, that we'd kidnap our own grandson?"

"Odd for you to put it that way," Mona said.

But Lucas spoke for her. "What reason would you have to kidnap the child when you can insert your own proxy into our very household? You'd install some … lackey as husband to ensure your own place in the boy's life?"

Ruth asked, "What kind of devious people must you be to suggest that we would do such a thing?"

"You two may speculate on our character as much as you please," Lucas said. "Your own characters are already fully understood, and your intentions made perfectly clear."

William and Ruth stood up and the Tillermans did the same, seeing them to the door. Ruth said, "I trust you won't use this to finally shut us out of our grandchild's life. We only want to be part of his or her family — "

"And you always will be," Lucas said, "we assure you. Thank you for coming by." With that, he closed the door and Mona fell into his arms. She hugged him like she hadn't hugged him in years, not since she was a little girl and her older brother Jack died quickly of cancer. She hadn't felt so vulnerable since then, not even at the news of Nathan's passing.

And she knew somehow that things were only about to get worse.

*

Ross held little Jesse in his arms, Liv serving Mona a plate of sliced honeydew melon and a glass of lemonade. Mona said, "I look forward to meeting him."

"I hope that you do," Ross said.

Liv glanced at him. "Ross?"

Ross could only shrug, wrestling to keep the squirming toddler in his grip. "Two good men are behind us, Liv."

"They may have been good men, but they weren't good for Mona."

"Two more different Amish men you could hardly hope to meet," Ross said, glancing at Mona. "One has to wonder what or who it is you're looking for."

Mona didn't want to think too much about it. "You say this new fellow — "

"Vincent, Vincent Yardeem."

"You say he's a pleasant enough man, and religious."

"I've never met a man of greater faith," Ross said.

Mona and Liv exchanged a nervous glance. "Then I suppose there isn't much more I could expect." Mona cleared her throat to correct herself, "Or hope for."

*

Mona had to marshal the strength to go to her next date, another daytime meeting in public. She didn't want any suitor to think he was being welcomed to make an untoward advance. But Mona also regretted the looks she was getting from the passersby, some of them neighbors or acquaintances from her earliest days in Adams County. Some shook their heads as they walked by the little table in front of the sandwich shop called *Darla's*. But sitting outside gave her an easy out. After her last dates, Mona liked the idea of being able to walk away quickly if she deemed her suitor unworthy, something which seemed more and more likely.

She'd been called *damaged goods* by one young man, *loose-lipped* by another, and Mona could scarcely imagine what she'd hear next. So she was relieved when she found a man of reasonable size and build, his face actually offering a warm smile that promised a tender heart.

She and Vincent Yardeem spoke mostly of their religion, and of the Bible, one of Mona's favorite subjects. They shared their favorite apostles; hers was St. Paul and his, doubting St. Thomas. They shared the stories of their families, their pasts, the odd circumstances of their shared present.

"The Lord took my parents when I was quite young," he explained, "in a plane crash, I'm sorry to report. Just another testament to our humble way of life. But they had to fly out to Boise for family business. I was raised by my uncle from that point, and together we keep a beet farm on the other side of the county."

"You and your uncle? That's not unlike Gil's story, isn't it?"

"Who?"

After an awkward pause, Mona shook her head slightly. "Never mind, an old friend. He's quite a well-known artist, he carved the up-stretched arm in the park down the street."

"Yes, I've seen it."

"It's quite good, isn't it? Done with a chainsaw."

Without losing his smile, Vincent said, "I found it to be quite craven, actually."

"Craven?"

Without losing his smile, Vincent explained, "First of all, it was done with a chainsaw? That's hardly in the tradition of the Old Order? There are hammers and chisels, no? Or does he favor the easy way at every turn?"

Mona had never even given it any thought, and doing so revealed little to be ashamed of. "The chainsaw runs on fuel, the electrical generator he sometimes requires runs on gas too. There's nothing uncommon about chainsaw carvings in either the New or the Old Orders."

"But it's part of the human body, and a naked part at that."

"That is true. But it's not a body, I don't think; better to say it represents the body of man, as in I Corinthians, the community being the whole and all of us merely parts … it's not meant to be … sinful or lusty."

"You don't know that."

Mona tried to suppress her growing ire. "As a matter of fact, I do know it. He's a very dear friend of mine, as I said."

"And I don't mean to insult him. But you *did* ask, after all."

"Yes, you're quite right I did. And I wouldn't have expected an answer that was less than forthright."

Vincent's smile returned. "That's a good sign."

"Perhaps I oughtn't ask so many questions."

Giving it some thought, Vincent answered with a quote from Matthew 6:8. "Your Father knows your needs even before you ask." After a long and strange silence, Vincent looked deeper into Mona's eyes and said, "And I know what you need, Mona Mol."

A bolt of cold dread shot through Mona's body and soul. Not wanting to know but unable to resist asking, if for curiosity's sake alone, Mona heard her own voice say, "And what's that?"

Vincent's smile dug deeper into his cheeks. "Why, to be saved, of course."

"Saved?" she repeated, stunned. Looking them both over, she said, "Vincent, we're … I'm Amish, aren't you? You're not some Baptist preacher in disguise?"

Vincent broke a chuckle and shook his head. "Of course not, Mona. But you, clearly, you've been touched by the devil's trident." Mona was so shocked to hear the phrase that she could hardly fashion a response. "I don't know what you did, and I don't judge you, Mona, not at all. We all fall short somewhere along the line. Likewise, we all should be ready to help our fallen fellows. And who better to do that than myself? Surely, nobody! God Himself must have intended us to find each other so we could each play our part in your ultimate salvation."

Mona asked, "You think that you can provide salvation, to me or to anyone?"

"No, Sister Mol, no! Only Jesus can purify, only Jesus can save. But I can prepare you, make you ready for Him, body and soul." Mona thought to barrage the man with a litany of insults, words that might reduce him in his own inflated vision. But she could hardly bring herself to do it and he didn't give her the time in any case. "My sister, you need to be saved, cleansed, purified, so that child inside you may be granted a better fate than that of the antichrist himself!"

"Oh now that's enough!"

Mona stood to storm away, but bumped straight into a familiar face, walking down the street in the other direction.

"Gil!"

CHAPTER FIVE

Vincent stood, a smile plastered to his face. "Well, well, the famous Gil."

Gil repeated, "Famous?"

Mona was quick to explain, "I was mentioning your carvings, the arm in the park … which work of art was that inspired by?"

"*The Creation of Adam*, from the Sisteen Chapel, painted by Michelangelo Buenarroti. The first, rare moment of union between God and Man."

"You enjoy the work of the Englischers?" Vincent asked.

"Some of it," Gil answered.

Vincent kept smiling. "More craven imagery."

"Some may think so," Gil said, "odd for one who has never seen to judge."

"God is the only judge."

Gil said, "Actually, according to Hebrews and other books, it is Jesus who will be the judge of the living and the dead, with Moses on one side and Elijah on the other."

Vincent stammered to fashion a response even as Gil turned to Mona. "I hope I'm not interrupting anything."

"On the contrary," Mona said, "in fact I was just hoping for an escort back to my buggy."

Gil extended his elbow and Mona slid her arm through. The two stepped away, leaving Vincent slowly shaking his head in pity and disgust.

They got only a few feet away before Gil said, "So it's true, what I hear." Mona didn't need to confirm the rumors, and she wasn't about to lie to one of her oldest and dearest friends. Gil went on, "I think that's very sensible, very practical."

Mona nodded. "That's what I'm told."

"Don't you believe that it's practical?"

Mona searched her mind for an answer, but she couldn't find it; the answer was in her heart. She said, "I … I don't think it is, Gil. I mean, to have a daed for the child, of course that's best, but … to go about shopping myself like a fattened pig at the county fair, I … I don't feel that it's what God wants for me."

Gil cracked a smile, inviting Mona's curiosity. He shrugged. "I didn't think so either." After a few more steps he added, "It does seem odd to me, somehow, wrong … to see you dating some fellow strange to you." Of Mona's head tilt, Gil explained, "After being with Nathan for so long, I mean."

"It does feel unnatural, I agree." Mona stared off, sad memories returning. "I never thought I'd be sitting across a table from anyone other than Nathan, though I suppose that was a mistake."

"No, Mona, you mustn't say that. Just because things ended for you and Nathan the way they did, doesn't mean that it was a mistake. We have to be thankful for every blessing we're given in this life Mona, and that includes every chore, every tear, every trial."

"I am coming to realize that these trials have their purpose, God's purpose. Your own aunt told me that God is rearranging things to His liking, so maybe … maybe things hadn't come together precisely the way God originally intended."

"That would mean that God had gotten it wrong the first time, wouldn't it? And how can that be?"

Mona was stumped as they approached her buggy, Clip-Clop huffing and shaking her head. "Maybe He didn't get it wrong, maybe … maybe we did."

Gil huffed out a little chuckle. "It wouldn't be the first time." Gil helped Mona onto her buggy, then gave Clip-Clop a little scratch under the chin. After a pat on the cheek

and a stroke of the mare's muscular neck, Gil gave Mona a
wink and stepped back to let her shake the reins and drive
the buggy off.

Mona didn't look back at Gil after riding off, but she
could feel that he was lingering, watching her go, thinking
about her every bit as much as she was thinking about him.
Is it true, she wondered, *is it possible? Could we three have
gotten it wrong as children and come together in a
mismatch?*

*Surely that's why I feel the way I do about losing
Nathan, so ... so cold and empty inside. I'm sad of course,
to have lost a friend and the daed of my own unborn child,
but that hollowness that was haunting me and still does, it's
because I never really loved Nathan the way I thought I did
as a child.*

*It was Gil I loved all along, but only God had the
insight to realize.*

Mona tried not to think about it, or to think about
anything or anyone else, but she couldn't. Even the tide of
conflicting emotions couldn't wash away this new yet
fundamental truth.

Gil, she thought to herself, just the name giving rise to a
warmth in her soul which she recognized as familiar but
which felt entirely, altogether new. Mona sat the helm of

85

her buggy, shocked at the truth that was staring her right in the face, and had been for ten years. Mona flashed back to all the hours of play, the moments of childhood romance between her and Nathan with Gil ever close by, silent and supportive. Mona's bile rose again, horror replacing her new joy.

How could I have gotten it so wrong? All these years with Nathan, I thought the love we had was the love we were meant to share. Was I misguided by Nathan's height and strength, his solid work ethic, his quiet and stalwart manner, those things we Amish girls are taught to admire?

But Mona couldn't help but smile to think about Gil's sense of humor, his unique artistic vision, the amazing creations he drew from God's own works and with God's certain blessing. She thought about how much Gil had lost, both parents and soon enough his aunt, and even more; the love of his life.

Mona wanted to cry just thinking about it. *Yet how brave and witty Gil remained,* Mona had to remind herself, *and still remains.*

Has Gil been suffering in silence all these years, bravely heartbroken but dutifully dignified? What sadness have I put him through with my childish and misguided affection for another? And what of Nathan? All our years together, I know he loved me like no other. Did I give him the best love I had to give, Lord? I never meant to be anything less than a good Amish wife and mamm, to give him the family and household we'd both looked forward to, Lord. If I was wrong or misguided, it wasn't deliberate. I never meant to shoulder Nathan with a loveless marriage, truly a fate worse than ...

Mona stopped short, even her imagined voice unable to say the word, or to think about what it meant.

Aunt Gerta said God was putting the members of the body where it pleased Him. And if it's true that we got it wrong, that I was wrong about what my feelings were, and for whom, did God have to offer me such a drastic correction? Is death the only remedy available to the Almighty? Noah and the flood, Sodom and Gomorrah, Exodus; God's punishments are swift and terrible, and woe to those who fail to understand His works.

But this only brought Mona to another worrisome notion. *What if Gil doesn't feel this way? Would he really be so hesitant even now? Was I not clear? I have to make my feelings known to him, without any question and beyond any doubt. But what if I do and he truly doesn't feel that way? Will he ever look at me the same way again?*

Mona swallowed hard as Clip-Clop stopped at a red light. Mona looked ahead and to each side, a crossroads opening up in front of her. In one direction was the path home. But the others would only lead her astray, deeper into the land of strangers, to be swallowed up and devoured like so many before her, and some so recently.

*

That night at dinner, both Lucas and Betty noticed Mona's preoccupation. Even little Charlie noticed it, glancing at Mona between bites of his oven fried chicken and scalloped potatoes. Beginning to feel conspicuous about being the subject of so many glances, Mona finally asked Charlie, "Have I got ivy growing out of my bonnet?"

Charlie shrugged. "You seem weird, that's all."

Betty said, "Charlie, language!"

But Lucas said, "The girl's right." He turned slowly to face Mona. "You had another of your dates this afternoon. What was the result?"

"It was … a mixed result, I'd say."

Lucas set down his fork, clinking against his plate. "Speak plainly, Daughter. I do not ask questions in order to receive riddles as answers."

Mona shrugged, quite innocently. "The young man won't be courting me."

"I see," Lucas said, raising a glass of lemonade to his lips. "I'll see to the necessary arrangements then."

"Well, no, Daed," Mona explained, "that's the mixed part, I guess. You see, I know whom I want to marry, the man I want to raise my child." Betty's expression brightened, brows high and mouth small. Lucas's spine went rigid. "It's Gil," Mona said, needing to add nothing more.

Betty smiled and leaned forward, extending her hand to cup Mona's own from across the table. It was all the reassurance and congratulations that needed to be passed between them.

Lucas was less impressed, rolling his eyes and letting his fork fall again.

Charlie said, "I like Gil."

Lucas said, "As do I. But he's … an artist."

Mona said, "He brings in good money to the community's coffers."

"But for how long," Lucas said, "until that chainsaw breaks and takes his arm off, or worse?"

Betty said, "Husband, really."

Mona said to Lucas, "Gil's a good man, a stalwart of the community, dutiful to his aunt, beyond reproach in his personal dealings. I've been friends with Gil all these years,

I know what kind of man he is." After a brief pause, Mona said, "I guess I did all along, I just didn't … I … "

Betty said, "These things happen in their time, Mona, in the Lord's time."

"And what about young Gil," Lucas asked, "I imagine he's already making the wedding arrangements?"

Betty smiled, but Lucas meant no humor in his remark. Mona glanced down at her plate, pushing the scalloped potatoes around with her fork. "Well, he ... we didn't exactly talk about it . in detail. I saw him today, that's what convinced me — "

"Just seeing him on the street made you fall in love?" Lucas shook his head. "That must have been some terrible date with the other fellow."

"It wasn't that, Daed. I … I've always loved him, as a friend … and Nathan, I loved him kind of the same way, or … or maybe our loves were slightly different. I think I had it wrong all the time, Daed, that Gil was the man I truly loved and was meant to be with."

"What about Nathan, rest his soul?"

Mona's mouth went dry. "We were young, confused, we made the obvious assumptions, everybody did."

Betty had to lean back in quiet guilt. "That's true, Husband. All of us as much as threw them together. It may as well have been an arranged wedding!"

"Now it's my fault?" Lucas turned his head away.

"It's nobody's fault," Mona said. "But God is putting things right, I'm certain of it. When I think about it, I feel closer to God than ever before, and I feel ... I don't know, I can't explain it, something deep in my soul — "

"Love," Betty said, "that's true love, my daughter, a love for the ages."

Lucas looked at his wife and daughter, knowing he had no more to say in the matter. He'd learned after long years of parenting that somethings were better left alone. So Lucas returned his attention to the plate in front of him, stabbing his chicken with his fork. "I will take a meeting with Gil, discuss the matter formally, see to the arrangements. We'll need to pre-empt the normal wedding season, considering the circumstances."

But Mona felt the blood drain from her face, and this drew worried glances from her parents. Betty asked, "What is it, Mona?"

"Well, actually ... "

Lucas said, "Mona ... " and needed to say nothing more.

Mona finally had to confess, "As I said, we haven't discussed it, Gil and I."

"You said you hadn't discussed the arrangements," Lucas said.

"And that's true," Mona said.

Lucas went on, "But you also haven't discussed … anything else of it, not even your *intention* to marry him?"

"No, Daed, it wasn't … the moment wasn't right. There we were on the sidewalk by the buggy, was I to announce my intention to marry him there and then? That wouldn't be very proper."

"No more improper than marrying a man without him even knowing it!"

"Oh Daed, you're being silly."

"I'm being — ?" Lucas calmed himself, breathing through clenched teeth. "You would at least agree that the boy has a right to know."

"Of course, Daed, of course, I … I just need to find the right way to broach the subject."

A tense quiet returned to the table as Betty, Charlie, Mona, and Lucas exchanged glances and Lucas returned to his chicken. "Do it at once, Mona. I'll be keen to hear how it goes."

*

Mona's mind and heart were fixed on marrying Gil. The more she thought about it, the more certain she was, and the more beguiled by her earlier choices. But the past was just that, and the future hinged on the present. Mona had a terrible feeling that, even though her paring with Gil now seemed like the most natural and Godly thing in the world, somehow it wouldn't be easy and it may yet prove impossible.

Could I be wrong again, Mona couldn't help wonder, *just as before, only worse?* Mona shuddered to recall the terrible correction God resorted to with Nathan's passing. *What would be the correction for this mistake, who will pay for their life next?*

That sad thought brought Gil's Aunt Gerta to Mona's mind. *The poor thing is already withering away,* Mona had to remind herself, *and she's really just looking for a reason to step out of Gil's way. Wouldn't Gil's finding happiness with me at last give her the excuse she needs just to let go? I couldn't bare it if our union had such a terrible effect. Perhaps seeing us together, setting off on a new family course, will give her reason to carry on, a family she can be an active part of?*

But Mona knew these were questions she could only ask but could not answer, that Gerta's life was not in her young and frail hands at all. There were other lives that were her responsibility, however, not the least of which was fast growing inside her womb.

And how will Gil take it? Will he think I'm just latching onto him for the sake of the child? When I tell him I love him for himself, my heart connected to his, however will he be able to believe me?

Nervousness swelled in Mona's belly, and she knew her body was reacting to more than just the pregnancy. But Mona determined to press on, convinced that this was the course God had set out for her, praying for the strength to see it through and the wisdom to follow it correctly and the grace not to fall over the edge and plummet into the chasm of her own doom.

Mona and Betty worked together to prepare a fine dinner of venison stew, green bean casserole, freshly baked biscuits with home-churned butter, and a fine, crisp dandelion salad with warm almond dressing served on the side.

Betty smiled at Mona as they packed the picnic basket. "They say the way to a man's heart is through his stomach."

Mona smiled. "Gil's no ordinary man." But Mona was praying her mamm was right anyway. The alternatives were too frightening, and too sorrowful, to consider.

CHAPTER SIX

By her cheerful demeanor, Mona didn't have to wonder too long about how Aunt Greta was going to react to the idea of Mona and Gil getting together. Though Mona hadn't said anything about it to either one of them, Gerta seemed to already know. She smiled as she came down the stairs to help Mona present the dinner, despite Mona's insistence that she relax. Gerta had waved her off, saying, "I've relaxed plenty."

And Mona was relieved, glad to see Gerta so revitalized, so ready to live again. And she suspected she'd need Gerta's help securing Gil's hand in marriage. She had no way of knowing how right she was.

They sat around the dinner table, the sounds of chewing and drinking filling the room with a wordless contentment. Finally Gerta broke the silence with, "This dinner is just delicious, Mona. You'll make some other lucky man a fine wife. You mustn't let the past interfere with the future, eh?" With a glance at Gil, she added, "And the future belongs to those who take it."

Gil glanced at her, nodded and returned his attention to the dinner. He said to Mona, "It really is delicious, Mona."

"My mamm did much of the work," she answered with a modest half-smile.

Gerta said, "I wish my nephew here could find a woman with a mere suggestion of your qualities." Her eyes drifting in Gil's direction, she said to Mona, "But he's so wrapped up in his work."

Mona said, "Mastery requires dedication, sacrifice."

"Still, must a young man sacrifice everything? There's still time enough to raise a family." Gil looked from Gerta to Mona, then back to his plate. Gerta went on, "I don't doubt that you'll find a husband before he finds a wife. Unless, by some miracle — "

Gil had been gulping down his glass and could finally interrupt with, "Oh, look at that, I'm out of milk."

"I'll get that for you," Mona said, but Gil was already standing and, with a smile and a shake of his head, disappeared into the kitchen. Once alone, Gerta looked at Mona and shook her head, rolling her eyes. Mona could only sigh as her worst fears began to come true.

Once Gil returned with a fresh pitcher of milk, the uneasy conversation continued. Aunt Gerta said, "I am ever amazed at how God does His works. You just can never tell what waits around the next corner."

Mona said, "Sometimes what you find ... has been waiting there all along, always by your side." Another tense silence followed. Aunt Gerta's body flinched just a bit, then Gil jutted forward, reaching to his shin under the table. His eyes went wide with shock and he looked at his aunt, open-mouthed but saying nothing. Mona very nearly broke out in a chuckle, piercing the tension in the room even if it didn't further the topic toward its natural conclusion.

*

Gerta insisted on helping Mona clean the plates and repack them into the basket while Gil locked up the barn. Gerta said, "I just don't know what it's going to take to get through to that boy. I don't know what's wrong with him."

"I think I do," Mona said, "but I'm not sure what I can do about it."

Gerta smiled, wiping the last plate and handing it to Mona to pack. "Love will find a way." Mona cracked a bittersweet smile. "You'll be fine," Gerta said, "the both of you. It'll be a relief to be able to go knowing that he's found the love of his life."

"No, Aunt Gerta, no!"

"Wait, you're not the love of his life?"

"No, I mean, yes, I am, I am the love of his life, and he's the love of mine. I've only now come to realize. How terrible that it took Nathan's death to … to show me the light."

"As I said, the ways of the Lord's works are mysterious, and they are sometimes painful."

"But they don't have to be for you, Aunt Gerta. We'll need you in our lives, to help raise our child. We want you living with us no matter where we are, and for a good long time too! You're only in your forties, Aunt Gerta, you could still find love yourself. You certainly have not lost your usefulness to the community, least of all to Gil or to me."

Gerta smiled, but her gaze sank away. "We'll see how things go. If it is God's will — "

"It is, Aunt Gerta, and God helps those who help themselves. It's not enough for God alone to act, for us merely to allow God to act upon us. As long as we act in accordance with God's purpose, we must act. We have to exert a will of our own to help God's Will come to fruition."

"The will to love," Gerta said.

"And the will to live."

Gerta gave it some thought, her distant gaze returning to find Mona's. They shared a nod and a smile, and both knew what each would have to do.

*

A few days later Mona returned to Gil's house, to Gil's surprise if not to his aunt's. Mona fond him in the backyard working on his carving of the flying flock of swallows. He was using an electric drill to reach in and file away the unwanted chips and burrs from the wings and beaks and the hardest-to-reach places. The drill was running of a gasoline generator, fumes heavy in the early summer heat.

He turned as if feeling her presence. "Mona," he said with an easy smile, lowering the drill. "No food? I'm not quite sure how I feel about that."

They chuckled. "I'm on my way to Adams County Medical Center for a checkup."

"Really, Englischer doctors?"

"Even Ulga Frau thinks it's a good idea, since I had my little spells. Anyway, I thought I'd bring Aunt Gerta along, have somebody take a look at her. Since she's getting so much better."

Gil gave it some thought, then nodded. "I've taken her to see doctors before, they were stumped. But I don't suppose it could hurt. If it makes her feel stronger, on the road to recovery, that's good enough for me. Let me clean up, I'll go along."

"That's not absolutely necessary, you've got a lot of work to do." She looked up at the birds, growing more intricate and lovely with the passing work. "I wish I could do something like this."

"You can." Gil handed her the drill, its bit actually a cylindrical metal file.

"Oh no, I mustn't."

"Just a little, to get a feel for it."

"Gil, I can't, I'll ruin it!"

"How could you?" Gil eased it into her hands and turned her gently to face the statue, the flock of wooden birds in frozen flight in front of her. Gil wrapped his strong arms around hers from behind, his hands on hers as he turned on the drill. The vibrations rippled up Mona's arms, her heart skipping with Gil's nearness to her combined with the drill's grinding power. He raised her hands, the drill between them, and with a strong and unyielding motion he dipped the drill bit into the wood. Chips jumped away, a little cloud of sawdust gathered as Gil rubbed the drill bit side to side, smoothing out the bird's underbelly.

Mona was flush and suddenly nervous, breath short and mouth dry. She wanted to let go of the drill and take hold of him with all her might, pull herself to him in a long and loving kiss. It was a moment she'd thought of more and more recently, but she'd stumbled into it unaware and now the very possibility was almost too much to resist.

But just as the temptation became too great, both she and Gil felt themselves approach that point of no return. Turning off the drill, Mona nearly gasped as she stepped out of Gil's embrace, a hand over her cheek to cover her fevered blush.

For his part, Gil stammered and fussed with the drill as it wound down. "I'll, um, I'll put this away, get cleaned up."

"Yes," Mona said, clearing her throat, "we don't want to … to be late … for the doctors."

"Right," Gil said, "the doctors, exactly."

*

Mona sat on that cold, metal examination table in the silly paper robe. She hated being there; but she reflected that, really, everybody else probably did too. It made her feel vulnerable, naked, sick, injured. And so deep in such a big Englischer building, Mona always felt separated from God somehow. She knew Him to be everywhere and all-powerful, but being in a hospital made Mona feel trapped, imprisoned, buried alive.

The notion brought a terrible image to Mona's conscience, that of Nathan's last desperate moments. *They couldn't save him,* Mona had to remind herself. But she shook it off. *They'll save Gerta though, or she'll save herself. We'll all be fine, I just know it.*

The doctor came in, wearing an unconvincing smile.

*

Gil repeated, "Tests? What do they mean, tests?" Gil and Gerta stood next to Mona, sitting in a wheelchair, a blanket over her lap and legs. "They just said they saw some things they didn't like; blood sugar, things like that. They want to run some test, have me here overnight for observation."

"But … what are they going to observe? What is it that they expect to see?"

"It's just to make sure I'm safe, I think, that I don't pass out again. Really, Gil, I don't think you have to be so upset."

"Upset?" Gil turned one way then the other, unable to step away from Mona but unable to remain calm. "I'm not … it's just that, you're perfectly healthy, there's no reason they should need to run any tests."

"They said it was fairly routine, nothing to be too worried about."

"*Fairly routine,*" Gil repeated, "*too worried.* You know what kind of things happen in these places, Englischer doctors and their accidents, medical mishaps … *Too worried,* how does that sound to you?"

Gerta said to Gil, "Take it easy, Nephew, there's no reason to upset yourself." With a glance down at Mona, she added, "Or frighten anybody … "

Gil glanced at Mona and then back at Gerta. "Of course, you're right, you're … it's just, I'm surprised that everything isn't, um, as it should be."

"We don't know that," Gerta said. "And if they're not, they can still be made right. It's never too late for that, eh, my nephew?"

Gil's gaze fell to Mona again and a little smile crossed his face. "Yes, I suppose that's true, isn't it?"

Mona knew why Gil was smiling, and she returned the wordless admission. They held hands, and Mona said, "Don't worry, Gil."

"What is there to worry about?"

Mona turned to Gerta. "I'm glad to hear you're doing so well."

Gerta waved them off. "They always did think it was all in my head, but what do they know?"

Gil huffed. "*Enough,* God willing."

*

Mona endured the poking and prodding and needles that were a part of her litany of tests. She didn't ask what every sample was for, what they were looking for or hoping not to find. She didn't want to know.

Her parents came to visit, little Charlie's big saucer eyes tearing up. After a tender promise to pick her up the next morning, they left Mona alone with her thoughts and prayers.

Lord, let my child be all right. I don't care about myself, not anymore. I know I've been selfish and childish, about who I loved and why. But I lay here as a woman trying to make the choices You would have me make. Is it already too late for me? Is my destiny already written out by Your hand in the pages of the Book of Life? If so, I won't beg for it. If You wish me reunited with Nathan, I will not resist. But Lord, I pray to you, and praise you for seeing my child safely to his first day of life, and then on to a healthy, long stay upon the Earth. What I have done, I have done in your name and with Your higher purpose in mind. If I have failed, I will pay the price, but do not ask others to pay it, not Gil nor his good and decent aunt, and surely not my little unborn child. I know you gave me this life in order to see it through, not to lose it terribly this way. I swear I never regretted this blessing within me, not in the horror of Nathan's loss nor in the revelation of my love for Gil. I never once felt ashamed or regretful, no matter how some around me may have felt. If I go to you, I will go with a clean heart and mind. But let me leave my child behind, to grow up strong and true and praising Your name for all of his or her days.

Amen.

*

Mona made it through a fitful night's sleep and woke up at sunrise. She was anxious to get out of that hospital. A big male nurse pushed Mona in a customary wheelchair across the lobby toward the exit, where Gil and Gerta and the Tillermans waited for her. Betty was the first to hug her, little Charlie not able to resist wrapping her little arms around her older sister.

"What about the tests," Gil asked, "what did they find?"

"They'll let me know tomorrow, but right now it looks like everything's fine."

"Praise God," Gil said, Gerta offering him a reassuring little hug.

"Praise him to the highest," Gil said with a relieved sigh. "Still, it's going be a long day waiting."

"Nonsense," Mona said, "we go on with things just as usual, just as they've always been."

But Gil seemed lost in a daze, eyes starring off as they followed her out into the bright sunlight of another new day. "Things as usual," he repeated in a mumbled mutter, "just as they've always been." After a moment, he added, "No, no more."

CHAPTER SEVEN

Mona was no more nor less shocked than anyone else when Gil dropped to one knee in front of the wheelchair just after the breeched the sliding glass doors. All she had time for was, "Gil?"

"Mona, I have to tell you this — "

Mona looked around. "Here? Now?"

"Yes, absolutely. It can't wait another minute. I've already waited too long, Mona, but I won't be fearful anymore. For years I've said nothing, it wouldn't have been proper. And even now, I know what some people might make of all this, but ... "

"Gil?"

Gil went on, "I love you, Mona Tillerman Mol, and not just as a friend, or as something like a sister, though you have always been both those things to me. But I am in love with you too, Mona, I've always been. All those years you were with Nathan, I thought you were happy, that he's the one you wanted to be with."

"I thought so too, Gil, I really did. Only now do I realize that … all these years, I've been with the wrong man."

"I never wanted to disrespect you or Nathan, or violate the bond you shared — "

"It was the bond *we* shared together, as friends. But — "

"We're more than friends now, Mona, and I want us to be that way together and for the rest of our lives. I want to marry you, Mona, and raise your child in a family we call our own." Mona was about to answer, but Gil interrupted with, "I know the timing is strange, but it's more than that to me, and raising your child more than just an … an opportune chance. I love you for you, Mona, I always have … and I always will."

Once again Mona was about to answer, but Gil went on to say, "I know it's not something a man should say in public, not an Amish man anyway. But I want the world to know, and your family as well." Gil stood and turned to face Lucas. "Mister Tillerman, your daughter and I are both well into our adult years; she a widow and with child. Still, I am willing to ask you for her hand in marriage, with all respect." Gil turned to look at Mona as she stood up out of the wheelchair and took Gil's hands.

Lucas glanced at Mona, a gentle smile on is usually stern lips. "I haven't heard my daughter accept your proposal. But if she does, you have my blessing."

Gil turned to Mona, whose eyes were already locked on his. From between her smiling lips, a single tear rolling down her cheek, she said, "Yes, Gil, I will marry you." Mona and Gil shared a happy gasp and then a deep, warm embrace. They'd always been close, but they'd never been so close, and they knew there would never be such a distance between them again.

Around Mona and Gil, Gerta and Betty hugged and Charlie looked up at her daed, rolling her eyes and shaking her head.

CHAPTER EIGHT

By the time the next Sunday came rolling around, the whole congregation was abuzz with the news of Mona and Gil. Few seemed surprised. But for the most part the community was enthusiastic and welcoming of their union. The idea of Mona raising her child without a proper Amish daed and traditional household had put the whole congregation on edge. The assuredness that no such blight would befall the congregation was a big relief to most of those who considered themselves involved.

Deacon Christoph read a sermon from I Corinthians 7, reading with special clarity the 39th verse: "The wife is bound by the law as long as her husband liveth; but if her husband be dead, she is at liberty to be married to whom she will; only in the Lord."

After the customary feast, the community met for fellowship in the backyard of the host family, in this case the Patersons, Irving and Mona and their brood of six children. Most people in the congregation were coming and going up to Mona and Gil, offering their best wishes with warm smiles and tender touches. Some kept their distance, including Vincent, one of the young men Mona recently dated once.

Among the congregation were the Mols, William and Ruth, though they like the others were separated during the sermon and the meal afterward. Once in the backyard together, the Mols seemed connected at the hip, Ruth's arm slipped into William's elbow as if forever leaning on him and he always at the ready to support her.

They walked slowly across the yard, earning plentiful glances from the community. They had everyone's pity, of course. But as Nathan's death receded into the past, it became more and more important for the Mols to move on with their lives. Death was a part of life, for the Amish community even more than others, due to their hard labor and minimal medical care. But that also made it all the more important to learn to live with death. Like television or automobiles, mourning could easily become a distraction which might replace God in the focus of the true believer.

But the Mols were still wrestling with their grief. And as they approached Mona and Gil and their united family, including Aunt Gerta, their misery was plain to see. It was also plain, to Mona at least, that their sorrow was only getting worse, and that she had much to do with that, despite her efforts to the contrary.

They all nodded and muttered their greetings as the Tillermans, the Mols, and the Durant / Frielings got together for the first time ever without one key member.

After well-wishes and condolences, William turned to Mona and said, "I wonder if we might not have a word with the happy young couple."

"You may," Lucas said, "and with us as well. Is it a family matter?"

William and Ruth shared a glance, then turned to Mona. "First of all, once again, my wife and I wish to apologize for any misunderstandings which might have occurred between us."

Lucas said, "Actually our understanding of the events you mention were spring-water clear."

"Husband," Betty said, "it's Sunday, after all."

Lucas shrugged and bit back on any response. William turned back to Mona and Gil. "We hear you are to be married, and of course we offer you our very best wishes. We know you'll be very contented together."

Mona and Gil both nodded and then shared a glance, letting the Mols continue with just the slightest bit of dread.

Ruth went on, "And, although we realize you'll be raising the child in your household, that you'll still allow us to be a small part his or her life, all of your lives. We want to be a big, loving family to the child, and we would be so grateful if you would have us."

Mona was quick to say, "Of course, you'll always be a part of my ... *our* child's life."

The Mols smiled and shared a little embrace. "God has truly blessed us all," Ruth said.

After a brief pause, William said, "And of course the child will know who the birth father really is." This inspired confused expressions to spread among the Tillermans.

Mona said, "I ... I hadn't given it any thought, but ... I never would have thought to lie to my child."

"Of course you wouldn't," Ruth said, turning to William. "Didn't I tell you?"

Gil gave it some thought. "I think it's a fitting tribute to our friend, that his memory should live on in his child by blood. I'd not have Nathan be forgotten."

William said, "Thank you, young man."

But it was Lucas who said, "Just a moment," increasing the tension among the families.

Betty said, "Husband — " but it was no use.

Lucas said to the Mols, "Don't you realize what you're asking? Not of Mona or Gil here, but of the child? You're asking this child to begin life born of tragedy, to go through life without ever having a daed he or she can believe in."

Gil said, "I believe in my aunt, but — "

"You knew your birth parents," Lucas said. "But this child will have to grow up with that sense of loss, that not you nor any man could fill. It's a crippling blow to your household, to the child's wellbeing. And why? To sooth their sense of loss, their sadness. But sadness is every adult's portion. I'll not have that misery hoisted upon my unborn grandchild."

William took a step toward Lucas, who stood his ground, the two Amish patriarchs staring each other down. "You persist in thinking yourself as above us in the child's lineage!"

"On the contrary," Lucas said, "I do not think of you at all."

After a tense silence, William said, "You haven't heard the last of this," before leading his wife away in a hasty but determined retreat.

Mona and everybody else knew they'd be back.

*

"What pretense," Lucas said, once more pacing the pine floorboards of his living room, Mona and the others sitting on the sofa, in the chairs, a tray of fresh fruit slices on the coffee table. "What nerve, to impress that upon us."

Mona and Gil exchanged a worried glance which wasn't lost on Betty. To protect them, Betty said to her husband, "Perhaps the greater threat to the child's innocence is to lie about who the true parent is?"

"I don't disagree that honesty is best, of course! But this is a truth most adults struggle to face. Look at how difficult it is for the boy's parents to let go. I say the boy should be protected from that truth for his or her own sake, and for the betterment of their new family." He turned to Mona and Gil. "You'll have other children, don't you want them all to feel as siblings, proper and true siblings? Do you really want that poor child to look into your face, young Gil, and see a different man than his own daed, in his siblings' faces features that are not his own?"

"I'd not have the child look into my eyes seeking truth," Gil said, "only to be refused that simple and precious thing."

Lucas shook his head. "You're an artist, Gil, interpretation is the lifeblood of what you do, it's God's gift to you. Perhaps this is the true purpose of that gift all along."

Gil said, "Lucas, I respect and appreciate your perspective, but — "

"Just give it some time," Lucas said, "give it some thought, see if you don't come around to my way of thinking." With that, Lucas stepped out of the house and into the kitchen, leaving Mona in the worried tension of her fractured family.

*

A week went by, July bringing the full thrush of summer to Adams County. Mona hadn't heard anything further from the Mol couple, and she and Gil had let the matter of Nathan's legacy rest as well, though it remained a matter of reflection.

Mona and Gil took Aunt Gerta into a local shopping district not far from the house. They needed toiletries and sundries and a few things they couldn't get from the farmer's market. But more than that, Mona and Gil were just happy to see Gerta so lively, so ready to get out and get on with the business of living.

They also could not deny enjoying the simple pleasure of being out with each other. There was no reason to hide their love, as the whole community knew and most were quite accepting. And throughout their lives, Mona and Gil had always shared each other's company as mere friends, albeit the best of friends. Now they could share even more, more than either had dared to hope for. It made everything else easier.

"I don't see how we can deny the child the knowledge of his or her true parentage," Gil said. "The truth will come out eventually."

Gerta nodded as they walked down the street, her eyes drifting from one storefront to another, savoring the dresses and fish tanks and other Englischer items she never would have given a second thought to before her illness and nearly miraculous recovery.

Mona said to Gil, "I do not wish to lie to my child, or to anyone."

Gerta said, "You will tell the child once he or she is old enough to understand. By then the love, the bond, between you all as a family will be set, and it will be unbreakable. Brother Tillerman will come to accept this, I haven't a doubt."

Mona couldn't help but smile, and she didn't want to help it. "You're so wise, Aunt Gerta, we're so blessed to have you with us ... that is, until you find a man and he marries you away!"

The three shared a chuckle, but it didn't last.

Mona noticed the Roland brothers, Peter and Paul, walking down the street toward them. They were staring right at her and Gil, and they weren't sharing the sheepish pouts of their previous visit. This time, they were scowling, snarling, eyes fixed on them as they approached. Peter shoved Gil with his shoulder, sending Gil stumbling back a bit.

"Pardon me," Gil said.

But the brothers stopped and turned to face him, Mona and Gerta quick to pick up on the new and terrific tension radiating out of the Amish brothers. "Peter, Paul," Mona said, "are you two all right?"

"Oh, there's nothing wrong with us," Paul said, looking Mona up and down, "nothing at all."

Peter added, "We're not the ones on our ways to hell, after all."

Gerta said, "I beg your pardon!"

"It's nothing to do with you, old woman."

Gil asked, "Then who … and what … has it to do with, Paul?"

"I'm Peter." But Gil didn't answer, he just stared hard into Peter's eyes, wordlessly demanding an explanation. So Peter explained, "And I think you already know." Peter turned and walked on, Paul by his side, leaving Mona, Gil, and Gerta confused and, for Mona, just a bit afraid.

*

Mona hadn't heard from Liv for a week or so, and she was excited to take the buggy to her place for a visit. With little Jesse too young to go to school, Liv spent most of her time with the child between chores, Ross working their vegetable fields in the back of the house.

But Liv didn't seem to share Mona's excitement. She poured the tea with a nervous tremble, biting her lower lip and answering questions with shrugs and one-word sentences.

"Jesse's getting nice and big."

"Not you," Liv said, "you're not showing at all."

Mona put a hand on her belly. "I feel like I've already put on a hundred pounds, or that I swallowed a whole turkey." Mona and Liv shared a chuckle, Jesse staggering around the house with a gleeful smile.

"You'll get used to it," Liv said, "even though it's only going to get worse."

Mona rolled his eyes. "Wonderful."

They laughed again, Liv saying, "It is wonderful, it really is."

Mona nodded, "I know, I do. So much to look forward to." They sat in a gathering quiet before Mona took a closer look at her old and dear friend. "Are you okay, Liv? You seem, I dunno ... out of sorts?" Liv turned away and shook her head, but Mona went on, "Really, Liv, you can tell me."

"No, I ... " But that was more than Liv should have said and she seemed to realize it. Under Mona's scrutiny, Liv shrugged, nervously biting her lip. "It's not proper, to spread gossip, when there's nothing to it, I'm certain, Ross and I both are!"

A hot worry grew in Mona's gut even as her skin grew cold and prickly. "Liv, what is it?"

"Well, Mona, and I say again that nobody thinks anything of it — "

"Liv, tell me!"

After a nervous pause, Liv explained, "Well, some people have been saying, I don't want to say who, but ... word's just sort of getting around ... "

"What word, Liv?"

"That you and Gil, well, how you two managed to come together like this, it's so ... ideal."

"It's God's work, of course it's ideal. How can they fail to see that?"

"Not just … how things worked out, but … I don't even know how to say it."

"Try, Liv, before I lose my lunch!"

"That you and Gil, that maybe … maybe the child you're carrying really is Gil's, and not … not Nathan's at all."

"But how can that be, Liv? I didn't see Gil at all until the funeral, and I was already pregnant by … " Then the true nature of the rumor became clear to Mona, as much as she wanted not to believe it. Mona sat there, mouth dry, head spinning with confusion and even more so with clarity. "They … people are saying Gil and I … had an affair?"

Liv could only nod. "But nobody who really knows you thinks it's true."

"But … who could ever even think to start such a horrible rumor?"

Mona didn't have to reflect long on who it was, or why they'd done it, nor on what she would do next; confront them.

Ross stepped into the room, quiet and sheepish. "I don't mean to have eavesdropped."

"Ross," Mona said, "you don't think I — ?"

"No, of course not. But my friend Vincent did say you went off with Gil, having met Vincent for a date!"

"That's right," Mona said, noting the defensiveness in her own tone. "Your friend Vincent seemed to think he was on a mission of my salvation. You should have heard the things he said to me. I suppose he's behind the rumors then."

"Actually, he mentioned to me that he'd heard it from somebody else." After a considered quiet, Ross added, "William Mol."

*

Mona assured Liv and Ross that she was going straight home, to calm down and consider her options. And she hated to lie to her old friend, but she couldn't resist going directly to her former parents-in-law. She felt God's strength welling inside of her, and she wanted to harness it whole she could and perhaps even convince them to reverse their terrible rumor if there was still time.

"How could you spread such lies?" Mona stood next to Clip-Clop and her buggy, William and Ruth standing on their porch, standing strong in each other's arms.

"We have said nothing which we knew to be untrue," William said. "You will have to be satisfied with that."

"But I most certainly am not satisfied!" Mona's voice rose with her ire, and she was past being able to hold either one back. "You must know in your hearts that I never cheated on Nathan, not with Gil or anyone else. I would never do such a thing!"

"We wouldn't have thought so either," William said, "with the appearance of wholesomeness you've always presented."

"Appearance?"

Ruth burst out, "But then you shun us, cast us aside!"

"Wife," William cautioned her, never taking his eyes off Mona. "We never would have imagined you would lie to our grandchild about his true lineage, try to wipe the memory of our only child from the community forever!"

"We wouldn't," Mona said, "we weren't going to do that, whatever my own daed wants. We were going to explain it to him, let him come around."

"More lies," William said. "Nothing you can say or do, or might have said or done, can be taken at face-value now."

Mona took a closer look at the two, hiding behind their Amish plains while working their very un-Amish plans. She said to them, "I know why you're doing this, so that you won't be disgraced! If you can't raise the child, if you think you can't see your boy live on through his child one way or another, you'd rather people thought the other, of me and the very child you claim to cherish! Look at the reputation you're shouldering him with, just to protect your own! I know that you're grieving for Nathan, desperate for some way to hold onto him or bring him back, but what you're doing is wrong and destructive!"

Ruth repeated, "Destructive? How dare you? You, who came into Adams County and turned our boy's head around, drove a wedge between him and his best friend, who you then also seduced — "

"Seduced?"

"You're wicked," William snapped, "and you'll not destroy this family, from roots to branches. We'll stand against you to the very end, to protect the Mols for generations past *and* future."

CHAPTER NINE

A week or so later, Gil stood so closely to his carving
of the swallows that Mona could almost lose track of where
it began and where he ended. He was so focused in his
work, eyes fixed on drill as he filed the wood down to
reveal the most minute detail. Reaching up toward the
bottom of one high-flying wooden bird, Mona couldn't help
but think of Gil's most famous creation, the arm carved out
of dead green ash tree in Harrison park. It had represented
the reach of mankind trying to transcend its earthly bond
and touch the Fingertips of God; like Gil himself, the
embodiment of that human struggle, moral and artistic, to
reach higher, to better know the Creator.

Gil turned off the drill and set it down, stretching his
neck and shoulders. He stepped toward Mona and gestured
for him to turn around so she could rub his shoulders
through his white shirt.

"It's coming along so well, I know the Bank of America
will be pleased."

"Their money will pay for Edith Arnold's skin cancer
operation, leave some left over."

126

Mona smiled, trying to resist the temptation of pride. To take her mind off of it, she said, "What about us? There are still arrangements to be made."

"Your daed and I will see to them."

"I beg your pardon? We're talking about selling a house, Gil, with mine the only name on the deed."

"I thought we'd let the renters take it over, raise our family here." After a pause, Gil added, "Unless you have some objection."

"Only to being left out of the decisions of my own life."

Gil gave it some thought. "Of course, that's you all right, and just the girl I fell in love with. Forgive me, Mona. Not even your husband and I'm already the man of the house."

Mona touched his cheek from behind. "You're already the man of my heart."

They stood in peaceful quiet, the wooden birds motionless in front of them, yet seeming to be constantly in motion. The shrill ring of the phone cut across the yard, a frightened kinglet leaping out of the royal oak branches and fluttering out over the valley. Mona felt a pang of concern shoot through her, but quelled it as soon as it struck. Mona still hadn't gotten used to using the telephone, and it had never brought her anything other than bad news.

Knowing how she felt, Gil said, "Probably B of A … to arrange delivery." Mona added, her heart already slowing back down to a normal pace as she followed Gil across the yard toward the shed.

In the rotting little shed, musty with mildew, Mona watched Gil's expression. When his reassuring smile melted from his face, Mona knew she'd been right.

More bad news.

*

Sheriff Ken Baller was waiting for Mona and Gil in Harrison park. Mona's heart sank to see the wrecked carving, sliced through near the foot of the trunk, a splintered strand rising up and barely connecting the carving from the stump.

"Oh Gil, I'm so sorry."

Gil sighed, trying to slough it off. "Nobody was hurt, that's what counts."

Sheriff Baller shrugged. "That's mighty big of you, Mr. Durant. I know this thing was vital to your career, brought in a lot of business."

Gil looked up at the sun. "It's almost noon, you're only finding this now?"

"Got a call about two hours ago, but this didn't exactly take precedence over the domestic dispute I had to deal

128

with across town. How many Sheriff's deputies do you think Adams County can afford? This ain't Columbus, Ohio, laddie buck."

"All right," Gil said, "I apologize. And nobody saw anything?"

Sheriff Baller shook his head. "Near as we can figure, someone came in with a chainsaw in the middle of the night. This being a business district, there weren't any witnesses, nothin'. You use a chainsaw yourself, don't you?"

Mona asked, "You think Gil would do this to his own work?"

The sheriff shrugged. "Just looking into all the possibilities. Is there anyone in particular you can think of who might have done this?"

"I can think of several," Mona said, "including at least one young man who considered this to be a craven image. And who wanted to date me but was ... interrupted by Gil himself."

Sheriff Baller said, "A love triangle?"

"Hardly," Mona said, "but he was clearly ... he felt rejected, he must have."

Sheriff Baller said, "I see."

Mona had to confess, "But there's more to it. Some people think, this young man among them, that I've been … less than an ideal Amish woman, as regards questions of … fidelity and … and pregnancy."

"Say no more," Sheriff Baller said, "I can see it upsets you. And in truth, I've already heard all about it."

"You have?"

Sheriff Baller nodded, glancing around. "Got a visit from a William and Ruth Mol, your former parents-in-law."

"They've been spreading the rumors," Gil said.

"It's not just that. They did come to me with the idea that you and their late son were … having marital troubles, let's just put it that way."

Gil asked him, "And what business would that be of yours?"

"None, as I told them. Your private affairs are just that. But the Mols had the notion that your … well, *extra-marital affair* is the legal term — "

Mona muttered, "Oh Lord — "

"That this might have been a motivation for some foul play on your part."

"Foul play," Gil repeated.

But it was Mona who said, "You mean … murder?"

130

Sheriff Baller said, "Actually, *homicide* is the legal term. But I wouldn't worry about that. What happened to your husband, it couldn't have been orchestrated by hand. To anticipate that he'd be alone, and that the earth would shift as it did, we just don't get seismic activity like that around here, you sure can't plan a murder on it. And if you really want to put any question of the child's lineage behind you, there are paternity tests you can take early in pregnancy which can answer the question without a doubt."

Mona gasped a little, Gil wrapping his arm around her for support. Gil said, "That we should even have to prove such a thing to these people, our friends and neighbors all these years."

"People gossip, especially in small town like this, where everybody knows each other. Can't be helped." Sheriff Baller went on, "And the Mols are ... they're not thinking clearly, I can't imagine. But that doesn't mean word hasn't spread halfway across the state by now. Any number of quietly angry people out there could have lashed out, almost anybody who ever knew your late husband. Then there are the wackos."

"The ... wackos?"

"Look, I know you Amish folks are plenty reasonable, I've lived here all my life. But I also know that some of

131

you, like anybody else, well, you tend to get a bit carried away. And with all the rumors and sour nothings swimming around you two, just about any Amish with a troubled or over-active conscience could have taken it upon himself, or herself, to stand up against you."

Sheriff Baller walked around the toppled carving. "Chainsaw, they're pretty common around here, no paint or other marks of vandalism, no real prints of any value. I'm afraid this could have been just about anyone, as far as I'm concerned. And let's be clear about this … I'm the only one who matters."

Gil asked, "How do you mean that?"

"Here's how, George Washington Carver; I get that this was probably somebody you know, somebody close to you. And I'll look into it, I really will. And I mean I will look into it."

Mona said, "Sheriff — "

But he interrupted with, "But as I said, I spent my whole here in Adams County, and I know how it goes with you folks. You're cloistered, isolated, and that's the way you like it. And that's fine with us, 'cept when you use our tax-sponsored emergency rooms and police services, but that's not really for any of us to decide, is it?"

"Then why mention it?"

"Why, Mrs. Mol? Missus Mona Tillerman Mol and soon Durant, because what we're looking at here is vigilante justice, at least as far as the perpetrator is concerned. And what I don't want from you is a vigilante response. Is that clear enough? I may not find who did this, I'm not going to lie to you. It's a simple case of vandalism and that's just not a priority for me."

Gil said, "What if it's more than just vandalism? What if somebody's sending us a warning, that things are only going to get worse?"

"We'll have to burn that bridge when we come to it. In the meantime this is a police matter and it will be dealt with as a police matter. Whatever satisfaction you do get will come from me, and not from any efforts of your own. I won't hesitate to arrest you, either of you, if I must."

Gil said, "We're not the ones who did anything wrong here."

Sheriff Baller looked them both up and down. "Keep it that way."

*

Mona and Gil were floored by what was going on. They were baffled by their choices until it seemed that they had none at all. It was a sad fact that they would probably have that Englischer test to prove to the busy-bodies and

133

gossipers of Adams County. Beyond that, they knew there would be little that they could do but push on and live their lives as they'd hoped.

"Perhaps it's for the best," Gil said as he piloted his own buggy across their little corner of Adams County. After reading Mona's confused expression, he explained, "Anybody would doubt you, doubt either of us, they're not really our friends. Our lives, our families, we'll be better off without them."

"Well that's fine, Gil, but … what about your carvings? Nobody here will ever darken your shingle again."

"My swallows will be in the Bank of America headquarters in Indianapolis. I'll get plenty of commissions from that. And where we fall short — "

"The community will help us? I don't think we can count on that, Gil. And it's just … it feels wrong, against the natural order of things."

Gil shot her an odd look. "You don't mean … us, that we're wrong?"

"No, Gil, not that, never! I mean … we're a communal people. Without the community, are we still Amish? What are we … who are we?"

"We're children of the God most high, Mona, and He loves us. With His love, and our own, what more do we need?" Mona couldn't argue with that, but it just didn't seem so easy, and she began to wonder if it would ever be as easy as she might have hoped. "What is it, Mona?"

"It's just … my daed was right about one thing; my child already has so much to stand up to, to overcome, and Ulga Frau hasn't even knocked on the door. A dead parent, now a false reputation — "

"We'll take the test," Gil said, "and we're going to see Ross now. Beyond that, we'll have to put it on the altar of the Lord."

"The Lord helps those who help themselves."

Gil offered her a reassuring smile. "That's just what we're about to do."

But Mona couldn't smile back. "I hope so."

*

"I don't understand this," Ross said as he took a seat on the arm of the sofa next to Liv, Jesse squirming in her arms.

"We just want you to let your friend know that we don't want any more trouble. We want to live in peace, we've done nothing to harm anyone."

Ross shrugged. "Why do you think Vincent had anything to do with it? He's a peaceable man, very religious — "

"Too religious," Mona said.

135

Liv said, "Mona, really."

"I'm sorry, but … that guy was just a wacko."

Ross repeated, "A wacko? What does that mean? Mona, what's come over you?"

"What -- ? This, Ross, all this! The last two months of my life have been crazy, and they're oly getting worse."

"That doesn't mean Vincent had anything to do with it."

"We talked about that very statue," Mona said, "he knew it was Gil's creation. He was insulted, clearly. But he's had his revenge and we just want to be left in peace."

Ross shrugged. "How can you think I'd associate with a person who would do such a thing?"

"We're not blaming you," Gil said.

"Stay out of it."

"I will not! How could you introduce a woman like Mona to such a fundamentalist?"

Ross stood to face Gil, Mona quick to put herself between them. "Boys, please — "

Ross said, "There are plenty of people in Adams County who would want to … express their disapproval, what you've done."

"We've done nothing wrong," Gil said, "there's a test that will prove that the child is Nathan's."

136

Mona turned to Liv, desperation growing in her cracking voice. "Liv, you said you'd never doubt me."

"And I don't, Mona, I don't."

"We're not the only other people in Adams County," Ross said. "The talk that's now going on about me at the farmer's market, where I found the very best men I could for his ill-conceived errand. And now I'm not about to go around making wild accusations at my friends based on your word, not after what you've put those poor Mols through." This caught Mona's attention, she and Gil both looking at Ross with new worry. He explained, "I don't happen to think you're treating them with very much sympathy or respect, and I'm not the only one who feels that way."

Mona said, "And I'm very sorry to hear that, but I'm afraid you haven't the slightest real idea of what you're talking about. You don't know the things they've said, hurtful and threatening, you don't know their hearts — "

"But I know my own, and it is with my family, my own family. I can't afford to have my neighbors turn their backs on me, my child can't afford it. You speak of the challenges your own child faces, what about ours? I'm sorry, but I just can't make the trials of your family the trials of my own."

Mona turned to Liv. "Liv?"

But Ross went on, "Don't ask her! I'm the man of this house, and I steer the course of things!"

"You're steering it straight into a pit," Mona said before she and Gil turned to exit.

Ross said, "If you want that bear back, you may have it! It will reside in the county junk yard by tomorrow night!"

CHAPTER TEN

The next day Mona took Clip-Clop and the buggy back to Gil's house to see how he was feeling after the troubling events of the day before. She knew he might need help retrieving that bear from Liv and Ross', if he was interested in doing such a thing.

"He can do what he likes with it," Gil said with a shrug as he went on treating the swallows carving with a tan liquid, spread from a can with a wide brush. "It's none of my affair." But Gil was distant, not as warm with Mona as he had been recently.

"Gil, is there something wrong?"

Gil broke a sad half-smile. "My aunt, she's been … backsliding the past few days, spending more time in bed, losing that … that glow that seemed to have returned of late."

"I'm sorry to hear it, Gil. She seemed to be doing so well. Should we take her back to the doctor?"

"They don't know anything, they say it's all in her head. Who knows? Maybe they're right. When things are going well, she was feeling better, but when the going gets a little rough … "

Mona put a hand on his arm. "You can hardly blame her, Gil. Look at all she's lost, how much she feels she stands to lose. Depression is a real disease among the Englischers, and in our own community too."

"I suppose."

"Then what she needs is reassurance, prodding, support; not pity, not to lay around letting every little thing get her down, right? And she needs somebody to offer that guidance."

Gil smiled, putting his own hand on hers. "You'll be such a good mamm to our children, I can hardly wait."

Mona put a hand on her belly. "Sometimes I wonder how long that wait will be."

Gil chuckled. "You've got seven months to go, let's not get ahead of ourselves."

"Excuse me?" Mona and Gil turned to see a man neither one recognized approach from around the side of the house. He was stooped a bit in submission, a white dress shirt under his tan face and Asian features.

Gil said, "State your business."

"Li Chin," the man said with an awkward smile, "from the Adams County Herald. You're Gil Durant?"

"I am."

"Well, I … I suppose you've heard about what happened to your carving in Harrison park, *Another Adam*."

"I have," Gil said, "and seen the damage for myself."

"Good, good," Li said, correcting himself to say, "I mean, it's not good, what happened, but … I would like to ask you a few questions about it."

"I have nothing to say."

"Well, you must have some take on it. That was your masterpiece, wasn't it? A very popular attraction around town — "

"The money it generated helped a lot of people in the congregation. So its true purpose had already been served. To put any more value into it, for me, would only be vanity."

Li nodded, raising a little recording device. "You don't mind if I record?"

"I told you I've nothing to say."

Li chuckled. "Really? 'Cause you're doing great so far. Do you have any idea about who might have done such a thing?"

Gil and Mona shared a worried glance, and Gil said to the man, "I think you'd better go."

Li looked at him, then at Mona, nodding in his defeat as he reached into his shirt pocket. He pulled out a business card and handed it to Gil, saying, "Here's my number if you change your mind."

Gil took the card but immediately dropped it to the ground without even glancing at it. Li understood the meaning of his gesture and smiled again. "Okay, I tried. Best of luck to you both."

Gil and Mona stood together as Li turned and walked away without another word. Once he was gone, Mona turned to Gil. "Gil, if we're part of his story we can include the results of that test, prove to everyone once and for all that you and weren't unfaithful to Nathan!"

"It wouldn't matter. They'll all believe what they want to believe. And to use them, the Englischer media, that will only turn more of our own community against us, against the child. It's for us to handle this within the community, for as long as we can manage to do that."

Mona nodded, but she knew there was at least one facet to consider. The sheriff had warned them not to get involved, and talking to a newspaper reporter was bound to upset him and his investigation, if there was one, and would turn the sheriff against them. And that was something both Mona and Gil knew they couldn't afford.

Something above caught her eye, and Mona glanced up to see Gerta in the window of her upstairs bedroom. She was back in her bedclothes, hair long and hanging down around her shoulders, pale skin bent in a sorrowful expression as she backed away from the window.

*

Mona was helping Betty with the laundry, hanging the wet white shirts and gray dresses on one of three long clothesline, wooden clothespins holding the garments in place.

Betty said, "I know that things will calm down soon, and Gerta will come around. I still think what she needs is a man of her own. Her life is too wrapped up with Gil's, I think."

"Still, I think there are some problems that a marriage can't solve. For some, marriages create more problems than they solve."

Betty had to nod. "I suppose that's true. I … I hope you don't look back on your own marriage to Nathan as that kind of experience."

"No, Mamm, of course not. I'm grateful for every moment with Nathan, and for the child he's left me to raise. He was a part of God's plan I should never regret. And you know we'll be sharing the full and complete story of the child's past, once that time is right."

"I know, and I think you're right to do so. Have you told the Mols?"

"They won't see me, and I don't blame them. I'm still struggling with forgiveness."

Betty nodded. "Time and faith will help to heal."

Behind them, Lucas said, "The injury may not be over yet, my family," as he approached from around the side of the house holding a copy of the Adams County Herald.

Betty asked, "Husband?" but she hardly need have done so. One glance at the paper in his hand warned Mona what news he was bringing, and none of it would be good.

Lucas glanced at the newspaper in his hand, giving it to Mona. "There's a story on your Gil's vandalized carving."

Mona was quick to say, "We didn't say anything to him at all, Daed. I wanted to, I admit, but Gil insisted that we not."

"The right choice," Lucas said. "You can see for yourself what they can do with the unkept tongue."

Mona glanced at the newspaper, her eyes scanning the article, mumbling the most relevant words. "'Amish chainsaw carver ... creation destroyed ... While the artist himself would not comment, other locals seem to believe the vandalism was anything but random. One source, a member of the Amish community who wished to remain anonymous, is quoted as saying, "We don't want their type around here, maybe this'll make that clear." When pressed to explain what the source meant by, "Their type," the source refused to comment. Other sources suggest an illicit affair with a local young woman and some suggest even participation in Satanic rituals.'" Mona looked up, her blood draining from her face. "Satanic rituals? They can't be serious!"

Lucas sighed. "A lot of people are given to … certain imaginings, ways of seeing things. They see the devil around every corner. It's a drawback to being so religious, for some."

Betty wondered out loud, "How could they not come to us to answer such charges?"

Mona said, "We told them we wouldn't say anything, I guess they took us at our word."

"No doubt they'd rather you not answer the charge," Lucas said, "the better to paint you with that bloody-red brush. But it may be just as well; the more you speak to them, the more you fan the flames they'll use to sacrifice you. We're not so far from the witch hunts of old, my family."

"But … satanic? It's just not like the Amish to think so hard on such a dark figure."

Lucas said, "They don't see it often."

"They're seeing what they *imagine* to be there." Mona shook her head. "What should we do?"

"I do not know," Lucas said, "whether we should do anything at all … besides pray, of course. Beyond that, the more we protest, the more guilty we all will seem."

"We shall pray then," Betty said.

But Mona knew she would have to do even more than that, and she'd have to do it soon.

*

It was only three days later that Mona was at Gil's to help see to Aunt Gerta. She was getting steadily worse again, and even Ulga Frau had no answer. All of her tinctures and remedies were wasted, as ineffective as the much-more expensive Western medicines.

Mona had tried to get Gerta to see a psychiatrist, but Gerta was insistent that it was more than just a waste of time. "They don't even believe God exists at all," Gerta had said, waving off the notion. "What advice can they possibly offer me?"

So Mona helped Gil sweep up the last of the wood chips from around the carved swallows, stopping often to admire its beauty. The birds seemed to be living, breathing, their outstretched little wings carrying them toward the heavens. Like the arm he'd carved in Harrison park, Mona recognized the common theme; small man reaching up to be closer to God, to escape the bonds of Earth; the birds, the arm. They were the same expression of Gil's inner desire for the things he never had and the things he would soon have in full, and for the rest of his life.

But Mona's blood ran cold to realize that there were no certainties in life, least of all a guarantee of happiness, no matter how worthy the recipient. *Not by works, but by His grace,* Mona silently reminded herself.

"It's a shame," Gil said, glancing up at the big carving.

Mona smiled. "Why? Lots of people will see it. We can always go out to Indianapolis and visit them from time to time."

Gil sighed. "Won't have to go much further than right out here, I'm afraid." Reading the curious tilt of Mona's head, Gil explained, "Got the call this morning. Bank of America read that newspaper story."

"Gil, they can't possibly believe the things that were printed in that article!"

"It doesn't matter what they believe, Mona. They said there was too much controversy now, they can't risk any ... *bad publicity*, as they put it."

Mona shook her head in disgust. "How can they do this? It's ridiculous!"

"We think so, but a lot of people out there, they'll be quick to jump to the wrong conclusion. What would follow? Protests, Christians pulling their money out of the branches all over the country, especially down south. Bank of America doesn't want any part of that, and I don't suppose I can blame them."

"Is that legal? Don't they still have to pay you?"

"There's something called a morals clause in the contract. Can you imagine, a morals clause ... in a legal contract, and *I* violated it!"

Mona leaned against Gil to offer her wordless support. There was nothing more to say.

Gerta asked Mona to take her back up to bed, and although Mona felt it was best that Gerta stay up, that she remain active for the rest of the day, Gerta almost fell over on the way across the living room, and Mona agreed to take her up to bed.

Once up in Gerta's bedroom, easing the aging woman in to bed, Gerta said, "It's true, you know. I'd doubted it for a while, but now, there can't be any doubt."

"About me and Gil getting together? How could you have doubted such a thing?"

"Not that," Gerta said. "Though I did doubt that for years, I see now that God's plan is perfect, and that you two will be together. It must be so!"

"And it will be, Aunt Gerta."

"Aunt Gerta. You really do treat me as your own family, so sweet and so pure."

Mona shrugged. "I suppose that depends on who you ask."

"I don't have to ask anyone," Gerta said. "I know what I know, I know what's true. And I know I'm leaving Gil in good hands, that you'll all be happy and healthy and — "

"Not this again, Aunt Gerta. You're not going to die! You have every reason to live; just because a few things have come up — "

"No, it's not that," Gerta said. "I knew before, that God was putting the members of the body where it pleased Him — "

"Yes, that's right. And where God is placing you is here with us, that's what will please God. This family is the body and you are a vital member! But you have to be strong, Gerta. I looked into this a bit, even went down to the public library. There's a thing called a *self-fulfilling prophecy*."

Gerta waved her off with a smile. "I'm no prophet."

Mona chucked, but it didn't last. "Not that kind of prophecy. It means that sometimes, and it can happen to anyone, that we're so sure something is going to happen, so worried about it, that it actually winds up happening."

"Such nonsense," Gerta said, "only God is the author of such things."

"God is the Creator, yes, but we must also do our part, Aunt Gerta. Faith without works is dead, after all."

Gerta's gaze drifted away, her lips forming a gentle smile. "Yes," she whispered, "yes indeed. But I want you to know that when I do go — "

"A long time from now," Mona insisted.

"Yes, a long time from now. But when I do go, know that will go in peace, and that I go knowing it is God's will that I go, that it is part of His great plan. I won't be sorrowful, and I won't want you to be sorrowful either."

A tear pushed down Mona's cheek. "The longer a time we have before you have to leave, the less sad I will be. Will that do?"

Gerta nodded, reaching out to Mona and gently wiping her tear away. "You're the daughter I never had, Mona."

Gerta pressed her palm to Mona's cheek, and Mona put her own hand over Gerta's, fingers intermingling. "I'm the daughter you'll always have."

CHAPTER ELEVEN

Deacon Christoph leaned back in his chair, the small plain oak desk in front of him. On the other side of that desk, Mona sat with Gil, Lucas, and Betty. Charlie was in school, and Gerta was home in bed, but Mona knew this wasn't a conversation that either of those two needed to hear or participate in.

Deacon Christoph said, "It is quite troubling, there's no doubt. On the one hand, those funds were earmarked for Edith Arnold's skin cancer operation. Our coffers are depleted for the next two months, but the doctors are very anxious that she not wait that long. These things can spread quickly."

Mona said, "Gil did his best. It's not our fault, what's happened."

"No, I know that," the deacon said. "But it won't endear you any more to the congregation. Especially given this … unfortunate turn of rumor."

"Isn't there anything you can do?" Gil asked the deacon. "Surely you don't believe this nonsense."

"No, I don't. But once these ideas take hold, it can be almost impossible to dislodge them." After a considered moment, he asked, "Have you given any thought to postponing the wedding?"

Lucas was quick to answer, "Why should we?"

"To let things settle down," Deacon Christoph said, his voice a calm contrast to the snap of Lucas's tone.

Gil asked, "Suppose they don't settle down? Anyway, should we send the message that we can be bullied by rumor and gossip, manipulated by the local newspaper?"

Deacon Christoph asked back, "Are those really the important issues?"

Gil nodded. "Considering what our child, what our entire family here will have to look forward to over the next generation or more, I'd say that they are indeed the really important issues! I say we do whatever we can to end this absurd rumor mill now, before it gets out of hand!"

"Gil is right," Lucas said to the deacon. "I see now that my daughter's instincts to use the media to broadcast their innocence may not have been so misguided. I realize that to fail to manipulate them is to allow them to manipulate you!"

"It's not too late," Mona said.

"It is," Gil said. "My career is already ruined. The truth is well beside the point, I'm afraid."

A long, still silence settled in the room. Deacon Christoph said, "There is another option." All eyes fell to him, and the deacon cautiously said, "Mona, you and your family came here about ten years ago, as I recall."

Betty said, "That's right. What are you getting at, Deacon?"

"I know it's going to sound odd and a bit off-putting, but perhaps another move might not be so disadvantageous."

Lucas tried to repeat, "Disadvan — ? Don't start speaking to us in Latin now!"

"He's saying we should move," Mona said.

Deacon Christoph said, "You've got each other, that's truly all you need. Perhaps a fresh start in another city ... or state, perhaps — "

"No," Lucas said. "We'll not run away from our problems."

Mona said, "We'd never be able to outrun those rumors anyway."

"And I'm not inclined to try," Gil added.

Lucas said, "Good for you, young man."

"I agree," Mona said. "That's not how we're going to raise our child."

"It could resolve a lot of problems for you," the deacon went on, "matters of the child's parentage, other ... economic considerations. You've still got one house you're renting to that nice visiting Amish family, you could sell it and the Durant home — "

"No, Deacon," Mona said.

Deacon Christoph sighed. "I know that, as I said, the idea is off-putting. And while you all may have your private reasons for wanting to stay, including sentimental, I urge you to think about the child's future, the ease or difficulty he or she will have to face, and at such a young age."

Mona said, "We do not intend to raise our child to value ease or shrug off difficulty. We'll raise our child to persevere, to stand up in the face of injustice and prejudice and not run away. No, Deacon, we're staying in Adams County and that's all there is to it."

Deacon Christoph nodded as he took in their grim determination. "Very well. In that case perhaps I can use my position to help enlighten our neighbors, the congregation, and see if we can't bring them around."

155

Mona was relieved that the deacon was willing to follow their chosen course of action, but she could not convince herself to be very optimistic for the outcome.

*

The next few days went on as normal, with Mona sharing her time between the Tillerman and the Durant homes. The third month of her pregnancy had just begun, and she was feeling the effects; the nausea, some tiredness, a bit of an ache in her lower back. But she also felt exhilarated, glad to be alive and to have a life growing inside of her. It drew upon her resources, but it gave her strength, courage to face whatever would come next.

But she could have had no idea how much courage she would need, or how soon.

Mona was sweeping up the living room floor while Gil was out beating the rugs. All was quiet, but there was a tension that Mona couldn't ignore. Once again she began to feel faint, her head starting to swim. *Oh no,* Mona wondered, *not again! Not now! What's going to happen now?*

Mona hadn't had a spell since just before hearing that she was pregnant, in that terrible moment she realized her love with Nathan had been misguided, not intended by

God. And there was the time before that, just before the sheriff arrived with the news of Nathan's death.

Her ears started to ring, her eyesight going soft, blurred, imaged ghostly around her. Bile rose in her stomach.

No, Mona told herself, *hang on, don't give into it! Don't let it get the better of you, not this time and not ever again! There's too much happening now, get a hold of yourself!*

Mona's head began to level, the room no longer spinning around her. The ringing in her ears subsided, her stomach calming and settling once again.

Then Gerta's scream rang out from upstairs, sending a bolt of fear shooting through Mona's body, her spine stiffening and her fingers squeezing the broom handle in her sweating palms.

Mona's arms and legs froze, but the echoing silence following Gerta's scream were even more paralyzing. She heard the back door open, fast footsteps getting louder as Gil approached, calling his aunt's name before even hitting the living room.

Mona's left hand regretfully reached for the white curtains and pulled them back. What she saw drew the breath from her lungs, and she could not even respond when Gil called her name.

157

In a flash, he was standing by her side peering out the window at the front yard. "Lord," he muttered, "help us all."

Gerta came staggering down the stairs, clinging to the banister. "What's going on, Gil? What do they want?"

"Go back upstairs, Aunt Gerta!"

"No, Gil, I won't! They must be a hundred strong, and they have guns!"

Gil rasped to Mona, "Take her upstairs, there's a Springfield in the coat closet near the stairs. I'll deal with them."

"No, Gil," Mona said, "my place is with you." Gerta had already reached the bottom of the stairs, her graying blonde hair matted and tangled, her face a twisted mask of fear. Gil looked back at Gerta and then at Mona, then out at the lynch mob which had come for him, far sooner that he or anyone might have imagined.

"Now's not the time for your modern independence, Mona, you're with child!"

"And I won't let that child lose his daed twice before he or she is even born! Gil, we're meant to be together, we always were. And that means through everything, no matter what. Together forever. We waited so long to finally be together, we came so close to living our whole lives in

158

quiet desperation. But I'd rather die than go on living without you, Gil."

"But our life is not the only one at stake, Mona!"

Mona glanced out the window, the scowling and familiar faces sneering, only a few guns among the crowed. "They know I'm with child, they won't shoot me."

"You don't know what could happen," Gil said. "I won't hide behind a pregnant woman."

"She's right," Gerta said, "our place is down here together, as a family." Mona looked at Gerta, and she knew what the older woman was thinking, the future she foresaw for herself, her moment of sacrifice presenting itself.

Mona said, "Maybe we should go upstairs after all, Aunt Gerta, not put any more stress on Gil."

"No."

"If we stay down here, we'll only be a liability, compromise Gil's safety."

But Gerta was already pulling the closet door open. She pulled out the rifle and tried to cock it. "Let's get this done," she said.

But Gil eased the rifle out of her hands and said, "You two be ready to go upstairs if needs be. I'll go out."

"No, Gil!"

"Mona — "

"What if they come in through the back?" Gil gave it some thought, knowing Mona was right. Muffled voices called his name from the front yard, and Gil took another look at Mona and Gerta. The two women glanced at one another, shared a nod, then looked back at Gil. They were resolved, and there was nothing that was going to separate them.

"Okay, we'll go out together," Gil said. "But you two stay behind me, is that clear?" The two women nodded, but Gil repeated even louder, "Behind me, at all times!"

"Yes, Gil," Mona said, "we understand."

Gil glanced back at the front door. "Okay then, let's go see what this is all about."

Gil pulled the door open slowly, the muffled muttering becoming more clear, hissing and booing rising as the three stepped out onto the porch, the sun's glare almost blinding. But Mona could still make out several familiar faces in that crowd, including the three young men Ross had fixed her up with; stern Albert Gretchinson and pasty Stan Larz standing on either side of righteous Vincent Yardeem. Not far from them, the Roland brothers Peter and Paul stood with William and Ruth Mol, proving to Mona the connection the four had long exploited.

"What's the meaning of this? My aunt is sick inside, this'll only upset her!"

William Mol said, "We're hardly here for her reassurance or comfort, boy."

"State our purpose then!"

Vincent Yardeem pointed a thin, angry finger. "To cast you out, back among the lepers and the scoundrels and others of your kind!"

Mona said, "You can't be serious! Why don't you listen to yourselves, you've gone mad with riotous rage, drunk with power that is not your own!"

"It's your master's power," Vincent shouted back, "we know you are merely his concubine!"

Gil said, "You're talking like fools! We're a religious people, and traditional, but we surely have evolved out of the days of the witch hunts of old!"

William called out, "The devil is older than any man, he pre-dates Adam and Eve! His power is no less alive today, and that is thanks to the likes of you!"

Gerta called out, "How can you believe such things? Were you not the same people who were convinced that it was an illicit love affair which blemished this family? Now you have another, more dreadful tactic? Why not just speak the truth? Several among you are prideful and shortsighted and are seeking to repair your standing in the eyes of others! The rest of you are merely swept away by it all, perhaps too ready to overlook your own failings in favor of imagining the failings of others!"

"You would say this," Ruth asked Gerta, "of course! You who benefits from so many of the boy's ghastly doings."

Mona said, "You're raving, Mrs. Mol, don't you see you've been driven half-insane with your grief?"

"We don't doubt the true nature of the child's parentage," Albert shouted from Vincent's side, "your falsified test results not withstanding. And we know this was the reason your heathen boyfriend set about to destroy Nathan, as he has so many others."

Vincent interrupted with, "The proof is clear for anyone to see, as we all see it. But let us suppose, Mona, that you are truly ignorant of what this man has been doing. You could have been tricked by him, the prize of his long-planned campaign. You wouldn't be the first woman to be so swayed. Remember Eve herself, in the Garden of Eden. But then again, Adam was no wizard!"

Gerta repeated, "Wizard? My friends, listen to yourselves! There's a line between religion and superstition!"

Vincent went on to Mona, "Then let us appeal to your sense of reason! Won't you challenge yourself, won't you open your eyes to the evidence all around you?"

"Speak it then," Mona said, "present your evidence, convince me!"

The crowd shared a mumbled muttering, eyes looking up at the three standing their ground on the front porch.

Gil glanced at Mona. "Stalling them. Smart."

Mona whispered back. "If they hear themselves in the cold light of day, perhaps they'll realize for themselves how misguided they are."

Gerta whispered, "And if they do not?"

But there was no more time for quiet speculation. Vincent called out, "As we said, we don't blame you, Mona. You'll have to pay the price or your sin, but we've not come to punish you."

"I said make your case," Mona said, louder and stronger.

Vincent stepped forward, taking the center position in front of the crowd. "Let's consider these … statues the man is so adept at creating. These are craven images — "

"You're the one who cut down my carving in the park!"

Ignoring Gil, Vincent went on, "Renderings of animals, the like of which are used in the dark arts, particularly of the Pagan variety, Druidism. What other function could these things have?"

"To celebrate the creations of God," Gil said.

"A convenient excuse," Vincent said, "when in truth they are key to your rituals, wherein you concur the spirits of the earth and the stream to do your terrible bidding!"

"Nonsense," Gerta said, the crowd hissing and shouting her down.

Vincent looked around at the crowd behind him and held up his arms to quiet them. "Please, friends, let reason prevail!" They did quiet, and Vincent returned his attention to Gil, Mona and Gerta.

Gil asked, "And what terrible doings am I guilty of?"

"Nothing less than murder," Vincent said. "You used your wicked conjuring to stop the Roland brothers' buggy, to prevent them from rescuing your intended victim. Nathan was your dear and close friend, you would have known he would have gone on to dig alone. Then you used your witchcraft to shift the earth and crush him to death. Did you envision it when it happened, Mr. Durant? Did you watch the murder from some reflective vision pool you have squirreled away somewhere, or did you simply feel the success of your murderous mission?"

Mona's stomach began to turn, visions of Nathan's death clinging to the back of her imagination. Vincent couldn't have failed to notice: "Yes, Mona, you see now what you're in league with, what terrors you had an unwilling hand in."

Mona snapped back, "I see nothing more than a confused, ignorant mob charging headlong into disaster!"

"Then look again, with a clearer view!" Vincent's voice became louder, more assured, the group rising up to groan and grunt their increasing agreement and dwindling patience. Vincent went on, "Did you not notice the remarkable rewards for his task? A ready-made family, the girl of his dreams."

Gerta said, "A ready-made family? Most Amish men would blanch, and even Gil here was hesitant, thanks to the likes of you with your pettiness and small talk."

William said, "Of course you deny it, as you are the succubus he is keeping alive with his sacrifices!"

Gil said, "Now that's enough. Say what you will about me, but leave this good and noble woman out of it!"

"We only hold you to account," Albert said. "The women are victims. But Mrs. Durant — "

"Feilding," Gerta said, "my last name is Feilding."

Peter Roland shouted, "Your last name is *mud!*" His brothers and others around him laughed menacingly, some spitting into the ground.

Vincent went on to Gerta, "Don't you find it strange that, with the death of one, comes the rebirth of another, and one closest to him? He's harnessing energies from one person to use on another. If that's not a trick of the devil, then Joshua failed the battle of Jericho. And with your waning health, old woman, we can only wonder who will be the next to be sacrificed to bring you continued life."

"I won't hear any more of this," Gerta shouted.

"What of your own sister and brother-in-law, the boy's parents, both now dead? Even the uncle has been taken, your own husband! You consider those coincidences?"

"Yes," Gerta said, "of course I do."

"She's in league with him," Paul shouted, "burn her, burn them all!"

The crowd cheered and lurched forward and Gil shot a rifle blast into the air, hoping to stop them in their tracks.

What happened next, happened quickly.

CHAPTER TVELVE

Bam! Bam! Rifle shots burst out of the crowd, tufts of gun smoke wafting around the muzzle flashes. The crowd scattered, ducking and shrieking. Mona clung to Gil, Gerta on his other side. But Mona knew instantly that something was wrong. Gil was heavy, unsteady in her arms before the Springfield dropped out of his hands and clang to a stillness at his feet.

He leaned into Mona with greater force, gravity pulling him down as the dark red stain spread across the chest of his white shirt. Her heart nearly burst behind her ribs as her lungs cramped for air they couldn't possibly find. Her throat nearly closed up, collapsing in on itself to release no sound, no breath.

Gerta said, "Gil," in a voice that was low and creaking, unable to reach him.

"Gil!" Mona shouted louder, her hands on either side of his face. He groaned, eyes half-open as the police and ambulance sirens got louder fast. The crowd was running in all directions, but their frenzy was nearly lost to Mona. She couldn't take her eyes off Gil's face, lips quivering as he

167

jutted, eyes rolling up into the back of his head, body quivering. "Stay with me, Gil, you hear me? Don't you die, Gil, don't you do it! Don't you die on me, Gil!"

By then the ambulance and Sheriff's Department cruisers were spilling into the property from the street. Deputies jumped out of their cars, screaming their credentials and firing their guns, ordering everyone to get down onto the ground. Many complied, others were already gone, and several others needed to be chased down and wrestled into submission.

But for Mona there was only Gil, his gurgled breath, his weakening grip in hers as the paramedics raced up and gently eased her aside. She gasped to be separated from him, reaching out with her fingers extended like Gil's carving, no longer standing in Harrison park. Mona and Gerta could only cling to one another as they strapped Gil onto a gurney and fixed him with an oxygen mask before sliding him into the back of the white truck, red lights still flashing.

*

As Gil's only direct family member, only Gerta was allowed to ride in the ambulance. One of Sheriff Baller's deputies drove Mona to Adams County General, and the Tillermans were called from the car. They took their buggy down to the hospital, and it wasn't long until they were all in the waiting room down the hall from the operating room. There was a tension among them which was increasingly common, a dark cloud which seemed to be ever-hovering over Mona and her loved ones.

Mona sat next to her mamm Betty, little Charlie on Betty's other side. Lucas sat alone, reading from a small copy of the Bible, his lips moving slightly as he read through all one-hundred and fifty of King David's psalms.

The operation was in its third hour, and Mona's hopes for his recovery were dwindling with every passing second. She'd prayed and praised for his recovery, but as the moments stretched out in front of her, in front of them all, her faith was slowly overtaken by desperation, and her hope by pitiful resolve.

Lord, is this really Your plan? You put me within a few feet of my life's true love for most of my life, then let me reach out and touch him only for these fleeting few months? What reason could you have for such a thing? Is it ... is it me? Have I displeased you in some way that I should be punished with the deaths of those around me? Whatever I may have done, I'll gladly stand for my own punishment, Lord, stand before You and whatever you deem right and just. But I ask that you not make these others suffer simply for the crime of knowing me, of loving me.

Mona's silent prayers were interrupted to see that Gerta was sitting across the waiting room, staring right at Mona with unblinking intensity. Mona was struck by a bolt of sudden panic, her heart nearly stopping behind her ribs.

Take it easy, Mona told herself, *don't weaken, don't slip now, stay in control. The Lord helps those who help themselves.*

Doctor Larson stepped into the waiting room, still in her green scrubs. Mona and the others jumped to their feet to greet the exhausted doctor, everybody asking at once as to his status.

"He's made it through so far," she said, a relieved gasp rising up from his loved ones. Doctor Larson went on, "We removed the bullet near his left lung, there was some excessive bleeding. We've got him sewn up, but he's going to be covering for a while."

Mona asked, "Is he in ... stable condition, or — ?"

"Critical, at the moment. When he wakes up, we'll see if we can't downgrade him to serious. After a few days, we'll re-evaluate."

"Can I see him?"

"Sorry, Mrs. Mol, only family in the ICU. Right now I think it's time you all went home and got some rest."

Lucas said, "Thank you, Doctor," as Dr. Larson stepped out of the waiting room. Mona glanced at the others, Charlie falling asleep at her mamm's side. Mona said to Betty, "You two take Charlie home, I'll stay here."

Lucas said, "You need your rest, Mona. Do not forget your own condition."

"I'm in a hospital," Mona said, "where better if something happens?" She could recall the horrible warning the doctor had given her, about the bad things which can happen in Englischer hospitals. But she just wasn't going to leave Gil, not then and not ever.

Gerta said to Lucas, "You three go home for a while, I'll stay here with Mona." Lucas seemed skeptical, but Charlie's heavy head made their decision for them. Betty gave Mona a kiss on the forehead and the three Tillermans stepped out of the waiting room and down the hall.

*

The hours passed slowly, Mona and Gerta sitting together, sharing wordless reassurance and jointly ignoring their creeping concern. Mona was exhausted, fading in and out of a fitful sleep, leaning up against Gerta for mutual support.

It was very close to dawn, but Mona could hardly tell. The lights in the hospital hallway were always on, it was always midnight in the garden of good and illness.

Gerta stood slowly from her chair, her eyes staring off as she turned and began shuffling out of the waiting room. Mona stood instinctively, concern pushing her toward the frail old aunt. "Aunt Gerta?" Mona felt her parents eyes following her as she followed Gerta out into the hallway, but they left the two alone.

"Aunt Gerta, what is it? I think the bathroom is the other way."

Gerta smiled, raising her old hand to Mona's face. "I'll be fine, dear." She turned, but Mona reached up and took Gerta's hand to keep her old friend their and facing her. Gerta glanced at Mona's hand, knowing what the younger woman's strategy was. Gerta said, "Remember what I told you."

"And you remember what *I* told *you*, Aunt Gerta. We need you!"

"I know you do, Mona, I know. And I'm not going anywhere. I'll be here as long as you need me."

Tears welled up in Mona's eyes, finally pushing out to stream down her cheek. "Really? You're not — ?"

"No, Mona. Listen to me, child; we'll all be together; one big, happy family."

"We will be," Mona repeated with a sniffle, "you and Gil and me and our child, all our children — "

"Yes, dear, yes." Gerta smiled, her own tear rolling down that withered, pale cheek. "I just want to see him, to hold his hand, to help him through." Mona didn't have to wonder or doubt. She herself wanted to do the same, and would have if she were allowed. But only family were permitted in the ICU, and Mona knew she was not Gil's family.

Yet.

She could only pray that she would still become that, as planned.

So Mona tapped Gerta's hand and slipped her own out of the younger's grip. "I'll be back soon," Gerta said with a gentle smile and a tender touch of Mona's cheek. Gerta turned and shuffled slowly down the hall toward the ICU, a small figure fading down that bright white hallway. She paused at the big double doors at the end of the hall, marked *Intensive Care Unit* with a sign with instructions and protocol. Gerta pushed a button on the wall and waited before a buzzer rang and a red light above the door flashed. Gerta pulled at the big door and, with a turn to glance at

Mona with a little wave, she stepped into the ICU and let the door glide shut behind her.

Mona stepped back into the little waiting room and sat down. She was alone in that ugly green-and-yellow room for the first time, and she felt just that way; isolated, adrift, apart from her home, her life, her family.

Is this the way it's going to be, Lord? Will I lose everybody I love, one by one, until I am alone with my child, the way poor Aunt Gerta is with Gil, just fulfilling my purpose and then wait bitterly for the release of death? Is that what life has in store for me, for us all?

A faint beeping leaked into Mona's ears from down the hall, settling deep in her heart. Her eyes shot open, the muffled scurrying and chatter from behind those double doors getting louder in the back of Mona's ears.

What's happening, she wondered, *what's going on in there?* Mona shot to her feet, but she was suddenly overcome with dizziness. Her mouth went dry, ears suddenly ringing. *Oh no,* Mona heard her own invisible voice echo in the back of her head. *It's happening again, as it always does just before ... just before ...*

The beeping and frenzy of activity in the ICU created a pang of sorrowful understanding to Mona's clouded thinking, just before her senses were overcome and everything went completely black.

Something's gone terribly wrong in the ICU.

And after that, there was nothing.

CHAPTER THIRTEEN

Mona came to after just a few minutes, the nurses all around her with their needles and their thermometers and their oxygen mask. Mona awoke to confusion, but clarity came fast. And the news was not surprising. Her spell had been in keeping with all the others.

It was bad news.

Doctor Larson decided to keep Mona at the hospital overnight for observation, though she seemed healthy enough and her pregnancy was not in any danger. Doctor Larson shook her round, chocolate-colored head, Lucas and Betty and Charlie standing around Mona's hospital bed.

"I've never seen anything like it," Dr. Larson said. "Missus Fielding came in and started praying, suddenly Mr. Durant's vital signs started failing. We did what we could, it looked like we were going to lose him. After a few minutes we were able to stabilize him again. We're still not sure what caused it."

Mona lay there, knowing what had really happened, not wanting to insult the doctor with a contradiction. Doctor Larson went on, "Then once we looked back at Miss

Fielding, she was sitting in her chair, hands to her chin …
stone dead. We tried to revive her, but it was no use." After
a perplexed shake of her head, Dr. Larson repeated, "Never
have seen such a thing. Anyway, you stay here the night,
we'll both keep a close eye on your boyfriend."

Lucas and Betty and Charlie looked at Mona, who
looked at her kid sister with an easy smile. "Charlie, you
needn't have come."

*

It was several hours later when Dr. Larson stepped into
Mona's room, interrupting Mona's reading of I
Corinthians, Gerta's favored verses about the parts of the
body being of the whole, placed just where it pleased God.
"Mona? There's somebody upstairs who'd like to talk to
you."

The doctor helped Mona out of bed and to the shared
room where Gil was had been moved once he was
downgraded to serious condition. He was groggy in his
bed, machines beeping and flashing behind his headboard.
He looked up and smiled to see Mona walking slowly up to
the bedside, Dr. Larson fading back into the hall to give
them privacy.

In a weak and craggy voice, Gil asked, "How are you?"

"Me?" Mona took his outstretched hand and pressed it against her cheek. "I'm not the one who barely survived being shot! You were so brave, Gil." Gil offered up a weak, drugged-out smile, eyes rolling up. "I'm so glad you made it through, Gil, so grateful to God for returning you to me."

Gil nodded, his fingers intermingling with hers. "Everybody played their part. I was thinking of you, y'know, the whole time."

"Gil?"

"I was in and out, light and fog all around, voices in and out, hard to make out. But I kept seeing you, imagining you, with your child — "

"*Our* child," Mona said.

"Yes," Gil agreed, "our child. And I just couldn't leave you behind, your love ... and my Aunt Gerta's love, were it not for that I don't think I'd be here at all."

Mona's heart skipped, her blood running cold. "Gil, about your aunt ... "

"She's gone," Gil said.

Mona fought back her confusion. "Gil, you know?"

"The doctor told me when I woke up, but ... I knew, I already knew. I could feel it, Mona, her strength pouring into me. I was being swept away, Mona, pulled away from you as if in an ocean, unable to resist the undertow. But I felt a ... a surge of strength, and I could recognize it as my aunt, the energy was ... familiar, loving. I couldn't think, but I knew; as much as I knew anything, I knew I had to fight to come back, and that she was giving me that strength ... down to the last."

Mona's memory flashed with the many tender moments with Gerta, that bold and courageous little woman. She recalled the conversation they had just before Gerta stepped into that ICU. *She knew,* Mona realized, though she suspected it even then*, Gerta knew what was going to happen.*

Mona said, "Your aunt told me more than once that ... if she went, that she'd go happy, fulfilling God's purpose. She felt so strongly that her life, and her death, would still have reason, meaning. And she was right, Gil, her death did have meaning, it was not in vain."

"I know, Mona, she was ... a remarkable woman, she saw more than any of us. She dedicated her life to me, gave her life for me." The two sat in silence, Mona holding his hand to her cheek, grateful tears running between their fingers. Something caught Mona's eye and drew her attention to the little window facing the street. A little blue swallow was perched on the ledge. Mona and Gil both glanced at the bird, which chirped so loudly and happily that they could both hear it through the glass. With a flutter of its wings, the swallow leapt off the ledge and disappeared up into the heavens.

*

Gil was allowed to leave the hospital for his aunt's traditional Amish funeral. He sat alone for the private service, and with Mona and the Tillermans for the second, public service. Gil was weakened and respectfully mournful, though Mona knew in her heart that Gil understood the sacrifice his aunt had made for him, for his future with Mona; and that she was happy and free and reunited with her own family in the Kingdom of God.

Deacon Christoph read from the Book of Psalms and other appropriate texts. But he also spoke directly to the congregation, in words both direct and necessary.

"Friends, we say goodbye to a good and dear friend, our sister in Christ, devoted to her family. Let us rejoice that she is returned to the presence of God, that she is at peace. And let any petty quibbles and suspicions lay with her, deep in the ground and no longer to tread among us. Her passing brings into clear view what is, not what we imagine might be. There is life and death and love, for one another and for God. There is labor and dedication, there is joy and there is trial and there is loss. We all endure them, and none of us ought cast aspersions on our fellows. There was a cloud of doubt over one household in our community, and that doubt brought chaos, havoc, eventually putting this poor woman into her grave! You cannot escape the consequences of the sin of gossip, of submitting to the temptations of our lesser selves! This woman died in prayer that her beloved nephew would live, and God granted her request. It is a blessed thing, a joyous but bittersweet sacrifice. But there is no darkness to it as some of you might imagine, nor was there any such darkness. That was born from the shadow souls of those too afraid to face their own iniquity, their own failings. They judged so that they would not be judged likewise. But this contradicts the very word of God, the sprit and the letter of His law! And there can only be shame and degradation for those who contradict God's Will; and chief among them is this: 'Love God, and love one another.'"

After the community viewing and the burial was the feast at the Baxter home at the foot of Resting Hill.

Mona and the Tillerman family stuck close to Gil, who was weak in his wheelchair. But he kept a courageous front, spine rigid in that hideous contraption. And Mona was gratified that he was still unwilling to back down from the ugly stares he and the others were receiving from the rest of the community. Most of the congregation hadn't participated in the mob scene in front of Gil's house. And they expressed horror and dismay at what the Mols and the others had done. Liv and Ross paid their respects to Gil and the others, and their regrets for the fight they'd been a part of.

"We never would have let things get so far," Ross said.

"You were right, Mona, it was a witch hunt. I'm so ashamed."

"I'm the one who should be ashamed," Ross said. "All three of my friends took part, one stood up as their ring leader? You both were right, I should never have imagined any of those fellows would have been a good fit."

"You tried your best," Gil said, "your heart was in the right place."

Mona added, "I asked for your help, Ross. Please don't feel badly." Ross tried to smile, but it didn't last.

And almost everyone who had participated in the mob did not come to the funeral, and for good reason. Paul Roland was in jail, facing charges of assault with a deadly weapon, perhaps even murder in the first degree. The Mols were so ashamed that word was they were considering moving out of Adams County altogether.

But that left the grim faces of over half the community, and they didn't seem so friendly or sympathetic. There was lingering suspicion in the air, even of the most ridiculous charges which had been leveled against Gil and the others. The mob had come and gone, but the grotesque notions of guilt and horror continued to fester among their neighbors, and it only threatened to blow up again.

*

The next few weeks passed slowly. Lucas invited Gil to move into the Tillerman home for his recovery. Although some would find it less than proper to have the man Mona intended to marry living in the house before the wedding, Gil clearly needed someone to help him get back on his feet. And Lucas was not about to let Mona live in his house unchaperoned, which would have been far worse.

The community was still resistant to Deacon Christoph's admonishments toward forgiveness. The money Gil would have made from the swallows would have paid for a skin cancer operation for Edith Arnold, which put a strain on the other members of the community to make up the difference.

"Some people resent all this upset and chaos," Liv said to Mona during a visit to the Tillerman house, little Jesse back at her house with Ross. "But I suppose they're just looking for something to be mad at you about."

"Will that ever end," Mona wondered aloud, "or are our lives here just … ruined?"

"Don't say that," Liv said as Betty brought some milk and cookies. "People will forget ... with time."

"It didn't take them long to forget that I've been here for ten years, I practically grew up here."

"Well," Liv shrugged, "there you go."

"What if I sell the house Nathan and I had, the one I'm lending to that nice family, the Greubers. If they'd like to buy it, the money could replenish the coffers and even go toward some repairs for those who feel … unfairly put-upon."

Liv gave it some thought and answered with an admiring smile. "So smart, such a worthy Amish woman. I know you'll yet be a pillar of the community."

"I'm glad enough just to be part of it," Mona said.

"I would have thought that other news story would have set everyone right, if the deacon's words failed to do so. It revealed everything about your innocence, made Gil out to be a hero."

"And you don't think he is?"

"After a fashion I suppose he is," Liv said, "a local hero anyway. I mean, the only true heroes are found in the Bible. But your Gil has proven his worth. I understand the town elders are taking measures to demonstrate their admiration for his courage and forthrightness."

"They needn't. But if it will help bring some patrons back to Gil's sculptures, that will only be good for the community."

Liv said, "I hear the Mols are finally leaving Adams County, and that will only be *great* for the county, and for you."

Mona gave it some thought, sad visions pulsing through her memory, and visions of even greater sorrows to come.

*

Mona went alone to the Mol home, taking Gil's horse and buggy and leaving Clip-Clop back at the Tillerman home. She rode the buggy up and didn't make it halfway to the house before the front door opened and William and Ruth Mol stepped out to face her.

Mona rode up to the end of the driveway and started to climb down from the helm.

"Do not bother to disembark," William said. "You're not welcome here!"

Ruth said, "We're leaving, and we're never coming back. You can have the child and do whatever you wish, we know we can't stop you!"

"But you don't understand," Mona said, "I'm here to stop *you* … from leaving." The Mols stood there, rigid and resolute. Mona went on, "I understand that you are mourning, grieving, that you were not in control of your senses. In that way, what happened, the things that were done or said, that really wasn't you at all; not the fine Amish couple who raised such a fine man as Nathan, not the stalwarts who could still be such an important part of this unborn child's future."

William and Ruth glanced at one another, still clinging and grim-faced. "How could you be so cruel," William said, "to force us through this kind of protracted humiliation?"

"No, Mr. Mol," Mona said, "nothing like that."

"You've already taken everything from us," Ruth said in a tearful, cracking voice. "You'd drag us through the mud, have us drag our crosses through the town square?"

William said, "Do not blaspheme, Wife."

Mona looked at the couple, still awash in their misery, blinded by their hatred for her, for themselves, even for

God. Mona said, "We used to be quite close, a happy family when Nathan and I were married — "

"But that's over now," Ruth said, "as your new life so clearly illustrates!"

Mona gave it some thought. "Is that really what this is about, you resenting me moving forward, still rejected from when I wouldn't turn my child or myself over to you? You can't really resent me wanting to raise my own child! Nobody will ever stand in the way of my doing that. I'm sorry for your loss again, and I offer you the chance, the welcome, the urging to participate in our lives, in raising the child. Nathan will not be forgotten, the child will know the truth. And the child and our other children should know you, and we can put all this horror behind us. That is my wish and Gil's wish as well. If you cannot bring yourselves to be humbled once again, even among your own or in the Eyes of God, then there's little more I can do. But if you leave, know that you leave with my forgiveness, my fondness, my love … and my regrets that I could not change your minds or soften your hearts."

No answer came from the still and silent Mols. The two stood there in that protracted silence before William turned Ruth back and led her into their house, closing the door behind them; as far as Mona was concerned, for evermore.

187

*

A week later Mona stood with Gil in Harrison park. Gil was slowly getting back to normal strength, his left arm still in a sling. The waning heat of August was already giving way to the oaky smells of the encroaching autumn. The park was filled with a crowd of about two hundred people, mostly but not exclusively Amish. The familiar newspaper reporter Li Chin was there too, a photographer next to him taking pictures.

Sheriff Ken Baller was also there, several of his deputies there providing a securing presence over the festivities.

Deacon Christoph himself stood beside the big form, ten feet tall, covered with a white sheet. "As a personal friend of Mr. Durant, I'm especially pleased to be asked to present his latest work. It was on this spot that Mr. Durant, *Gil* as we know him, created a unique wooden carving from a tree growing in this very spot. It was a popular, even beloved contribution to our community until acts of short-sightedness, mischief, even wickedness brought it down forever. But Gil has endured, transcended their ill-will. And now we're all here to mark that fact, to celebrate it, to thank Gil here for being a lifelong part of our community, and to look forward to many more years of his God-given gifts."

188

The crowd applauded, Dr. Larson also in attendance and clapping enthusiastically.

Deacon Christoph went on, "There were complications to Gil's life, one was the destruction of his carving, and another was the subsequent rejection of yet another statue, one he created for a well-known banking concern. It seemed a sadness that they decided against accepting it. But for us it has become a joy, because Gil has donated the piece to the county, and now we have put it here in the very spot where his other work stood. It is, perhaps, all the more appropriate."

Deacon Christoph pulled the sheet off to reveal the carving of the flying flock of swallows. It was elegant and airy, rich in detail and realism. The crowd offered up a gasp and then a furious round of applause. Mona turned to Gil and offered him a gratified smile, her hand on his arm. Gil couldn't suppress his smile, as much as he tried. He looked up, a happy tear in his eye.

*

The next Sunday services were being held at the house of Jann and Wilma Burke and their four children. The community was still enjoying the thrush of excitement from the unveiling of the statue. Everyone agreed it was a great honor to God and to His creations, and to the gifts He

189

bestows upon the faithful, that Gil could render them with such skill. Nobody doubted that it would be even more well-appreciated than the other carving, and that it would keep Gil's carving career healthy and productive for years to come.

After the sermon and the feast, the congregation was happily collected in the Burke's backyard. Liv and Ross and Jesse joined the Gil and the Tillerman family, and the conversation flowed easily once again.

"After the wedding," Mona explained to Liv, "I'll move into Gil's house and we'll raise our family there."

Gil turned to Ross. "You'll have a new grizzly bear before then."

"You needn't bother," Ross said. Off of Gil's confused expression, Ross confessed, "But you could help me raise mine up out of the mud I buried it in. I'm sure it'll be fine."

Gil smiled. "It may be a bit the worse for wear, but maybe you've devised a new finishing technique."

They shared a chuckle, but it died away quickly. He turned and Mona followed his line of sight. Only a few yards away, William and Ruth Mol were walking across the Burke's backyard and toward them. Everybody in the congregation was watching them, not a word being spoken as a tense silence grew like a bubble.

Nobody doubted that the bubble was about to burst; just how terribly ... and violently ... was anybody's guess, but they had only seconds before everybody in attendance would see for themselves.

CHAPTER FOURTEEN

Gil stood protectively in front of Mona, but she gently stood her ground by his side. The whole yard went silent as William and Ruth Mol presented themselves to Mona and the others.

"State your purpose," Gil said, to nobody's rebuke.

William cleared his throat and pulled back his shoulders. "We have come ... to beg your forgiveness." A hushed gasp rose up from the congregation, everyone coming in closer to better hear the Mols' words.

Mona said, "I've already forgiven you — "

"But we did not ask," William said, "and we must!" William looked around to the others, now a crowd fully surrounding them. "We humble ourselves before all of you with equal humility."

"Forgive us our sins, friends, we ... we were beguiled in our grief, blinded by sorrow, in that way ... not ourselves, not the people who stand before you."

Mona was gratified that they'd taken her words, and her sentiments, so much to heart.

But William went on, "Still we stand to answer for our sins, and to confess them here and now, for all to know. We knew in our hearts that Nathan was the father of the child, that Mona and Gil never acted in anyway untoward. She was right; we were hurt, felt shut-out. We were anxious to prevent any ill-will against us, but instead we have earned that very thing, seven times worse than what would have been."

Ruth looked at the crowd around them. "We let ugly assumptions be made, even fostered them along, things we knew were untrue. In this way we caused that riot at Gil's house, and the terrible fate which befell poor Gerta Fielding. We are guilty of her death as if we'd put a gun to her head and pulled the trigger ourselves!"

"That's not the way the Englischer law sees it," Lucas said. "That should be enough for any of us."

"But it's not enough for us," William said. "We felt it was better simply to leave, not to dishonor you, our good and noble friends and neighbors, even the whole of the Amish community. But beyond that, and behind that, was our shame, our disgrace. That was our true reason for leaving, but we know now that we would never be able to escape that sorrow, that horror. No matter where we went,

God would know, and we would know, and you all would know."

Ruth added, "It was Mona who showed us the way, the true nature of real Amish grit. We tried to chase her man off, but they stood their ground. We are humbled to follow in their footsteps, and we would be grateful if you all would forgive us and welcome us back to your ... to *our* community."

Mona stepped toward her former parents-in-law, everybody in the congregation watching and waiting. Mona broke a smile and opened her arms to them, William and Ruth falling gratefully into Mona's arms, and then the embrace of the whole Tillerman family. The congregation threw up a mighty cheer and converged on Mona and the others, everybody slapping their neighbors' backs and enjoying the communal good feelings of reunion, of healing, of wholeness.

Once the topic faded from the crackling conversation, everybody started to think about the next big event in Adams County; the holy matrimony of Mona Tillerman Mol and Gillard Horrace Durant.

*

Mona and Gil's wedding was held in mid-September, months before the traditional post-harvest season. But everyone agreed it was more important that Mona and Gil be married as soon as possible. And once the community was united, mid-September was as soon as was possible.

They did hold a traditional service in many ways traditional: It was held on a Thursday, a service much the same as would occur on any Sunday. It happened in the bride's family home, Lucas and the Tillerman family pleased to host their friends and neighbors for such a joyous occasion.

After the service, the benches were put together to form tables for the wedding meal. The mixture of bread filling and chicken, mashed potatoes, cole slaw, apple sauce and creamed celery, knows as a *roast*, was a highlight of the feast. Leafy celery stalks were put into jars as the centerpiece of table. Pies, doughnuts, fruit, and pudding were served as desserts, along with hot coffee and tea and milk for the kids. There were also several wedding cakes, one made by none other than Stan Larz as a gesture of apology.

The Mols enjoyed being taken back into the bosom of the community. After the feast Mona and Gil stood and looked across the yard, the congregation once more in happy union, though perhaps not so happy a union and

Mona and Gil were enjoying, and knew they would enjoy for the rest of their lives.

Mona was struck with a bolt of fear, a sudden nausea which seemed to burst in her belly. Goosebumps rose on the backs of her arms, and Mona's head began to swim. *Oh no,* she cried out silently in the back of her mind, *not now that things are going so well! No, I won't allow it, I won't let it happen!*

Mona exerted all her strength, teeth gritted. Her hearing went dull, her focus blurred, heart pushing cold blood through her veins. But she stayed on her feet, knees quivering beneath her.

"Mona," Gil said, the whole family looking at her with new and grave concern. "Mona, are you all right?" Mona held on, the trembling already passing, hearing and vision quickly returning. "Mona?"

"No, it's … I'm fine, Gil, fine."

"You're sure?"

"Yeah, Gil, just a little … tired, it's been such a long day, and I am in the family way, after all."

"You sure are," Gil said with a little smile. "Let's get you out of the sun." Gil led Mona back toward the house, but Mona caught sight of old Ulga Frau, the local midwife, glaring at her with a grim intensity, worry in her ancient, leathery face.

A cool breeze raced up Mona's spine, clouds rolling in from the east.

Autumn was approaching fast, and nobody in Adams County or anywhere else was safe from its ravages. Mona knew that, and she braced for what was coming, ready to pray and praise for God's mercy and protection. But she knew that alone would not be enough, and she wasn't sure if she had the strength for what lay ahead.

*

Autumn did come to Adams County, and it brought the bright orange and purple and yellow of the changing maple leaves, the woody scent of pine in thickening morning haze. Midwife Ulga Frau was sure to visit Mona often as her pregnancy continued, but there seemed to be no cause for alarm. Beside Mona's brief spell months before, there were no signs of danger.

Gil's injuries had healed by the harvest in early November, and he volunteered to help the neighbors gather their pumpkins and eggplants and cabbage heads. He and Ross worked side by side gathering his potatoes and vegetables, the two men forging a stronger bond than they'd enjoyed before. Gil's forgiveness had won Ross' respect, and Ross' own mistakes had humbled him.

Mona was ripe with child, her round belly growing by the day. It was harder and harder to help Betty with the chores, but she insisted on doing what she could. In preparations for the big Thanksgiving feast, there was too much to do for her or anybody to slough off. She stood by Betty every step of the way, preparing the turkey, making the stuffing, cleaning and stripping the green beans for the casserole.

And when the big day came, the Tillerman house was filled with laughter and good cheer. William and Ruth Mol brought oven-fried chicken, which had been Nathan's favorite. It was their first Thanksgiving since he'd passed, and Mona could see that, from time to time they would glance at one another and share moments of spent grief. But the merriment and family around them would quickly pull them back to the celebration of life and community which brought them all together.

Liv and Ross and Jesse came too, along with their own surviving parents, who brought hand-churned maple iced-cream. But that would have to wait.

Mona sat at the end of the big table next to Gil, and they smiled at one another frequently, wordless exchanges of love and gratitude. Mona was tired, her appetite spoiled, but she assumed that was due to all the hard work preparing dinner. Betty and Lucas kept glancing at her, but people were doing that more and more as her pregnancy progressed. Pregnancy was a difficult time for a lot of women, a lot of Amish women in particular, and with Mona's history of brief fainting, people were growing protective and for fair reason, so Mona didn't think much about any of it.

Lucas asked Gil, "How goes your carving? You're clearly strong enough to get back to it."

"And anxious to," Gil responded. "A friend has a fine piece of redwood for me, almost ten feet wide and twelve feet tall."

"Just think what must be waiting inside that wood," Mona said, "ready for your vision and your chainsaw to liberate it."

"God puts the figure there," Gil said, "I'm lucky ... and blessed ... if I can find it."

Mona couldn't help but smile. *How true,* she thought, *for us all. And in my own life, how blessed I am to have found what God placed there for me. And I will always be grateful and ... careful that I remain ... remain worthy ... that I remain ...*

Mona began to sway, her eyes staring off, a slight tremor vibrating upward from the back of her brain. Her body was shod with numbness, eyesight blurring, ears ringing.

Gil reached out to her, his grip on her shoulders barely registering to her confused senses. A lump rose in her throat, blocking off any air, and it seemed to Mona as if the entire room was spinning, tilting, upwards until it threw her off her chair.

"Mona!"

CHAPTER FIFTEEN

Mona's eyesight went black, her body trembling as they laid her back on the floor. She could sense the panic around her, make out their whispered worry, hurried footsteps leading to the back of the house and to the phone shed.

Gil slapped her face, harmlessly but hard enough to register and hopefully bring her around. She felt it but could not respond. It was as if she were half-asleep, dreaming that scary moment when the limbs are too heavy to move, the voice too weak to scream.

What's happening to me, Mona asked herself in that dizzying frenzy, *am I finally dying? Did you hear my prayer, Lord, that I myself should be punished for whatever sins have offended You? If so, I won't defy you, but ... what about my child, Lord, must that poor life also be lost, before it's even begun? No, Lord, I beg you not to take this life I carry, this blessing You bestowed upon me. You can take away my life, but this innocent creature need not suffer, Lord.*

Or are you sparing the child even more pain to come?
Is Your plan to remove us all from this world, one by one
until we're all gone and forgotten? Why, Lord, why?

Mona could sense the activity around her, the sirens
blaring, being strapped onto a gurney and fitted with an
oxygen mask. *Foolish Englischers,* Mona couldn't help but
think, her body immobile among the scramble to save her
and her child. *Only God governs life and death, only God.*

No, Mona had to contradict herself in that timeless
moment, the ambulance racing toward Adams County
General, and a final accounting. *It's not God alone. He*
creates life, yes, but it is ours to preserve if we can, ours to
sacrifice if we must. Aunt Gerta proved that the will to live
is as important as life itself, that one can sacrifice or simply
abandon life if the will is strong enough, if it is in
accordance with God's mighty will.

And I want to live, I want to stay with Gil and the others
to raise this child and so many others, to go on with the
blessings the Lord has bestowed. I want to, and I will if I
can, Lord. And I know You will not think me rebellious or
wicked. You want me to fight, Lord, just as you wanted
Daniel to face the lions and Jesus to face the Pharisees,
Pilate, the might of Rome herself. This is a trial you've
prepared me for, I see that now. My other spells were

merely tests, to prepare me for this ultimate struggle. And struggle I will, Lord, knowing that You are not my enemy or my jailer, but my loving Father, my liberator, my One True Love.

Gil's fingers just barely registered as being wrapped around hers, his voice cutting through the din and buzz in her ears.

"Don't you die on me now," Gil said, echoing word she had said to him in his own time of peril. "I love you, Mona, so much, and you love me, I know you do. We're married now, Mona, that means you have to stay with me, do you understand? You promised, you swore a vow!" A terrible silence passed, Mona unable to explain that their vow ended with the parting of death.

Gil went on, "You're going to be okay, you're going to come back to me so we can raise our child together! I know you will, Mona, I know it!"

Mona could sense the ambulance slowing to a stop, the muffled sirens no longer drilling into her dying ears.

"Okay, we're here at the hospital, Mona, we're here and the doctors are going to take care of you now, you hear me? You do, Mona, I know you can hear me!"

I can, Mona wanted to cry out, *I can hear you and I want to be with you, because I love you so much, Gil, I always have and I always will!*

"I know you love me, and you want to stay here with me and live the life we've waited for, that we've earned!"

Yes, we have earned it, my love. But it is not by our deeds, but by His grace that we are redeemed. I will stay if I can, but if I cannot, I do not want you to weep or mourn for me.

"We've been though so much in so little time," Gil went on, his voice cracking with desperation, "you can't give up on me now, on us, I won't let you!"

I never would if it were my choice, my love, my own heart's own. Stay with me for as long as you can, and I will do the same.

"Don't worry, my love, I'm not going anywhere, I'll never leave your side; not now, not ever."

Nor will I ever leave you, even if it seems that we must part. I'm not going anywhere. I'll be here as long as you need me.

"Keep fighting, Mona, keep fighting! You've never backed down from anything or anyone in your life, don't you back down now!"

Hear me, Husband, even if I cannot speak. Feel my words, know my truth; we'll all be together; one big, happy family.

Mona could sense the gurney being raced down a long hall, double doors clacking open. Instructions were muttered from one to another, a familiar voice cutting through the others.

A paramedic said, "Her water broke on the way in!"

Another said, "She's fading fast, Doctor!"

But Dr. Larson snapped back, "Take her into OR 2 for a cesarean section, I won't lose them both!"

"Cesar — " Gil tried to repeat, "no! What are you talking about?"

"I'm going to have to ask you to step back now, sir!"

"I won't! I'm her husband!"

"You'll be her widow if you don't step back and let us do our jobs, sir!"

So it's true then, Mona silently said, *I am to die. But my child will yet live, Lord? Tell me I will not die in vain.*

Mona felt Gil's hand around hers, others trying to pull him away. But his fingers resisted, their last bit of strength feeding into Mona's hand, as if the very pulse of life were flowing into her. Mona lay there with visions of Aunt Gerta, willingly pouring her own last bits of life force into

205

Gil to revive him. He'd said he'd felt it in that crucial moment, and Mona's scrambled consciousness could feel it too, a tremor of that resurrection power which had passed through the Christ Himself, the gift of God's love which had rolled away the stone and released that greatest gift mankind had ever or would ever receive.

Mona could feel Gil's urgent love in their still-clinging hands, and that of Gerta as if reaching her from another plane, another place. And the power grew stronger, more familiar, traces of Nathan's own undying spirit reaching out and contributing to the stream of love and hope that might yet bring Mona back to consciousness, back to the world of the living, delivered there from the world of the loving.

It was the will to live, and the will to love.

But they could not do for Mona what she knew she alone would have to do for herself. *Don't let go,* Mona urged herself, *don't let Gil's hand slip away. Hold it tight and never let it go! Squeeze with all the strength there is, all the power of those gone before and He who is yet to return. Hold onto that gift, that holy blessing, and never let it go!*

"Sir," Dr. Larson said, "you have to back away now, before I call security!"

206

"No," Gil shouted, "she's squeezing my hand, she's coming around!"

"You're going to break her fingers, Mr. Durant!"

"I won't let go," Gil shouted, "whatever you say!"

Don't let go, Mona urged, *keep holding me, hold me tight forever! Hold me and pull me up and together ... together we can ... together ... forever ...*

Mona gasped, her eyes shooting open, mouth panting and pulling in frightened oxygen, head darting in every direction.

Gil, where are you? Gil!

Then she saw him, standing next to the gurney in the crowd of nurses and technicians, strange faces bent in expressions of amazement; eyes wide, mouths small and dipped open.

"Gil," Mona tried to say under the plastic mask. She weakly pulled it down to gaze up and into the tearful eyes of the love of her life, her husband and soulmate. "Gil," she said, again, too weak to say more.

And Gil could say nothing through his twisted grin, tears pouring down his cheeks. There was nothing he could say and nothing which needed to be said.

Doctor Larson asked Mona, "Mona, can you hear me?" Mona nodded. The doctor asked, "What's your name, hon?"

"Mona Tillerman Mol Durant."

The doctor said to one nurse, "Okay, cancel that operation, let's get her into maternity, stat!"

"What are you saying," Gil asked, "what does that mean?"

Doctor Larson looked at him and Mona and calmly answered, "It means you're about to have a baby."

"No, not now," Gil said, "it's only seven months, it's too soon!"

"Tell that to the baby," Dr. Larson said. "Now are you coming with us or not?"

Gil looked down at Mona and she up at him, their hands still clasped. The doctor needn't even have asked.

*

The labor took several hours, but Mona and Gil became the grateful parents of their first child early the next morning. They named the boy Nathan, and he was greeted by a large and contented family. Once the child was released from the premature ward of the hospital, William and Ruth met the Tillerman family in the lobby downstairs as Mona made her last trip out of that hospital in their customary wheelchair. But this time she was leaving with a family, whole and in tact; it was a life just as God had designed it, all the members of the body were precisely where it pleased Him.

A blustery December wind pushed across Adams County as Gil escorted his bundled wife and baby into the buggy for the brief ride home. As they rolled that chair toward the waiting buggies, Mona glanced upward, an astonished smile spreading across her face. Gil followed her line of sight up into the thickly clouded sky to see a flock of blue swallows, small and brown and numerous, the flock flying this way and that and then back again.

William and the others also looked up. Betty said to Lucas, "Shouldn't be any swallows, not this time of year. They're all down south."

But Gil and Mona both understood. Mona said, "Nathan always used to say they looked like a hand waving … "

After a bittersweet moment, Gil asked, "Waving goodbye?"

Gil put a hand on her shoulder and Mona put her own hand on his. She said, "Or hello." They shared a tearful smile and climbed into the buggy, their extended family filling the it and the other before they rode off together to a new and happy life of loving each other and loving God.

Made in the USA
Lexington, KY
25 May 2017